BIOWEAPON Eclipse

By Kristen Hartbarger

bioweaponeclipse.com

Table of Contents

CHAPTER 1

A figure strode down a steel hallway. He was clad in a green sleeveless trench coat, a light green jumpsuit, and green open-toed boots. He walked upright like a man but had the features of a wolf. His body was covered in thick brown and tan fur. Alert triangular ears adorned the top of his head.

A fluffy tail swayed back and forth behind him. On the ends of his fingers and toes were sharp claws. The lupine humanoid, a therian, stepped into a dimly lit room.

"You called for me, father?"

A white-furred wolf-therian sat on a throne on a small platform with stairs leading up to it. His outfit was much like his son's but far more embellished, and in black and gray. "Yes. My intelligence network tells me that the body of Dynamo had been recovered and taken to earth by smugglers five years ago. Your mission is to locate Dynamo and destroy him. Understand?"

"Yes, father. I will not disappoint you," the brown wolf-therian assured with a gleeful grin full of teeth.

"You'd best not," his father warned, flashing his own fangs. "Now... assemble your Elite and go. It's already been five years, there is no time to waste."

"Yes, father." The brown wolf-therian left the room, traveling down the hallway. He activated his comm-link, which was hidden in his ear, concealed by the fur. "Azura, Neva, Jaron, Kyrie. Be ready to leave. We're going to earth." A chorus of affirmation, some eager and some not, came through the comm before he turned it off.

Five years, huh? Sounds like father needs to get a new intelligence network if it takes them that long to find out something that important. The resistance is probably involved; they're a tricky bunch, especially with that Rubi. She'd make a fine addition to our team. … It's strange, though. It's been five years and Dynamo hasn't returned to finish what he started. Hope he hasn't gone weak on me.

The Martian terrain was calm without a dust storm in sight. The normally orange sky shone blue as the sun set. A lone building stood on the surface, a large storage facility. No roads led up to it but there was a path worn in the dirt. It was surrounded by a barbwire fence and guards that stood around it.

An explosion blew out part of a wall, and then another and another. The structure started to crumple and burst into flames. Guards ran screaming, not knowing what to do. Some were crushed under the rubble or consumed by the flames.

"Where is she?" A figure was overlooking the demolition from a cliff through a pair of binoculars. He was dressed in rusty camouflage and wore a short cloak. His long, slender tail flicked back in forth in anxiety.

A cloaked figure burst out of the collapsing building; a bushy red tail was all that could be seen clearly. She quickly made her way up the cliff and crouched next to the other to watch her handiwork. The fox-therian wore a black kitsune-styled mask with magenta markings that covered her face, the eye holes filled with orange glass.

"Another victory, another weapons depot the regime won't get to use. Good work, Rubi," he congratulated her. "Unfortunately, they can rebuild faster than we can take them down."

Rubi looked around the cliff, pointy ears shifting in all directions.

"What is it?" the gerbil-therian asked. "I don't hear anything."

"Marin," Rubi responded in a whisper. "Where is she?"

The gerbil joined in her search. "I don't know. She was here. Maybe she... wandered off."

The corner of Rubi's lip curled up and her ears turned backward as she heard a strange but familiar noise. She turned to see a five-foot midnight purple disc hanging in the air just above the ground, seeming to distort the world around it. A therian woman with blue fox ears and three blue fox tails stepped out, dragging a small badger-therian girl with her.

"Marin!" Rubi exclaimed, raising a fist in front of her. "Let her go!" Her fist promptly burst into orange flames.

The blue fox girl wagged a finger at her. "You know better than to threaten me with fire." A small flicker of green flame danced on her finger before going out. "If you want her, you'll have to come get her." She jumped backwards back into the portal, yanking the badger along with her.

Rubi wasted no time in running after her.

"No! Rubi, wait!" the gerbil shouted, but it was too late. Rubi had already disappeared into the disc, which shortly disappeared itself.

"No..."

Red dust blew across the Martian landscape. The sun was setting, a blue glow in the otherwise tawny sky. An armored figure wrapped in a rust-colored cloak stood against an army of therians decked out in protective gear and armed to the teeth with advanced weaponry. The armored figure gripped the hilt of his sword, itself an advanced weapon, preparing himself for the onslaught. He leaned forward, readying for battle as the creatures neared his position.

"For earth."

He bolted; sword held out at his side.

"For my family."

He swung his sword, slashing a blaster in half, the barrel hitting the ground. He made a fist with his free hand, electricity dancing around it, and slugged the soldier in the abdomen. He slashed at another.

It wasn't long before he was surrounded, completely overrun by the enemy. They were starting to get in shots. His cloak was full of holes. The integrity of his armor was failing. It had been failing, having faced hoard after hoard.

He fought on, ignoring every blow. Enemy after enemy fell to his blade. All their numbers weren't enough; enough to stop the android.

Dust blew over the fallen bodies, the armor-clad android still standing. Surveying the scene, he walked on, using his sword as a cane. For how long he walked, he didn't know. His internal clock had long ceased working.

The android could see nothing, but the barren landscape. He was far from any civilization. His vision became hazy, fading in and out.

"I did it."

He wobbled, losing his balance. His vision faded further. The android fell forward onto the red dirt. His vision flickered out, now seeing only blackness.

"I did it..."

An android modeled to have the appearance of a young man was lying in bed, a space-patterned sheet half kicked onto the floor. A power cord was plugged into a spot on his chest, the other end in an outlet beside his bed. His eyelids blinked open, revealing crimson eyes. He ran his fingers through his jet-black hair and groaned, "Why didn't I set my wake time to an hour later?"

After a few moments of debating whether to return to sleep for another hour or not, he sat up. He sluggishly reached for the plug in his chest and pulled it out, tossing it to the side. He grabbed a circular flesh-tone disc that looked almost like a thermos lid and screwed it into the short cylindrical hole in the center of his chest, covering the port that the charge cord had been plugged into.

He swung his legs over the side of the bed and pushed himself onto his feet. He turned around and made his bed, smoothing out the creases on the sheet. Satisfied with that, he stepped into the bathroom. An android had no real use for a bathroom, but the house came with one adjoining every bedroom. In any case, he could store things there rather than have it take up space in his bedroom.

He quickly combed his hair and changed out of his pajamas. He threw on his clothes for the day: a pair of cargo pants, a T-shirt, and a light jacket. The android left his room and walked down the large stairs that led into the entrance room.

This room was littered with trophies and awards for achievements in the field of robotics lining the shelves and framed on the walls. The carpet in front of the door was the only spot that showed any signs of dirt. Shoe racks were next to the door, one on either side of it against the wall. The android selected his shoes and plopped them on the carpet. He slipped his feet into them and left the house.

He ambled over to the garage, only attached to the house by a canopy over the walkway. He stepped inside the man door and pushed a button on the wall to open the garage door. He pulled a set of keys out of his pocket and hopped onto a red magcycle, a motorcycle that was propelled by electromagnetic force, having dynamos in place of wheels which also enabled the vehicle to hover above the ground.

He started it up, pulled out of the garage and hit the button to shut the door. He pulled out onto the road and drove on. After about maybe twenty minutes, time which he made pass quicker by listening to the radio, he arrived downtown. Shops and restaurants lined the road on both sides. Cars were parked all along the side of the road. People were walking down the sidewalks, busy on their way.

The android parked his magcycle and made his way to a café. Once inside, he scanned the seats. His gaze stopped on one where a young woman with cobalt blue hair and caramel skin was sitting.

"Marcus!" The woman waved as he walked over. "Just a little bit late, as always. So much for having a clock in your head."

Marcus just laughed, well aware of his ironic habit of showing up fashionably late. "Yeah, well, we'd better order before they run out of muffins."

"Oh, well, we wouldn't want that, now would we?" She stood up and followed him to the counter, placing her order. Marcus placed his after hers and paid the cashier. They moved along the counter to wait for their order.

"One iced coffee, one cappuccino, a chocolate chip muffin, and a cherry muffin?" the man behind the counter at the pick-up spot asked.

"Here," Marcus answered. He and Azura took their muffins and drinks, then returned to their table. The android took a sip of his cappuccino before asking, "So, are you going to the convention tomorrow?"

"I suppose. Don't see why you're going, though. It's not like you're going to be on display."

"Well, no. Not, like, officially anyway," Marcus agreed. "But it's more than just a bunch of tech displays. There'll be venders and food and... well, it's just a big social event. You've had to have heard of it before."

"Of course, I've heard of the Mecha City Tech Convention. I've just never been," Azura said. "and they only focus on the tech displays on TV."

"Ah, I've never watched it on TV." Marcus took another bite of his muffin before remembering that he wanted to tell her something. "Oh, yeah! I had this weird dream."

"Hmm? Go on."

"I was... well, someone was on Mars; I'm not sure who it was supposed to be. Anyway, he was in battle armor and had a sword, and he fought against this huge army of Chimera and beat them, but he collapsed later from the damage he took in the fight." His hands gestured wildly as he told the tale.

15

"Dreaming of being a battle 'bot, are we? I thought you wanted to be a starship captain," she teased.

"Don't be ridiculous. Our ships don't travel far enough for that to even be a real job yet."

"Yet," she repeated. "You're an android. Maybe you'll live long enough until they invent deep space travel."

Marcus chuckled. "Yeah, maybe." His attention turned to a vibration in his pocket. He excused himself and pulled out his phone, reading the text sent to him. "It's Mom. She wants me to help set up the booth at the convention center. Sorry."

"We can resume another time," she stated, her way of telling him not to worry about it.

Marcus put his phone away, grabbed what was left of his muffin and drink, and stood to leave. "See you tomorrow then?"

"Tomorrow," she agreed with a wink and a grin.

He turned and left the café, leaving Azura behind. She watched him leave, waiting until he was out of sight to pull out her phone and typed out a message, sending it. Azura remained there to finish her breakfast.

It was well into twilight, rain pelting down on the city from the ashen sky above. An armored red figure darted down the sidewalk and into an alleyway, metal feet splashing through the puddles. He halted, looking over his shoulder, fists ready to defend against whomever was following him.

"Where did they go? And what do they want?" he muttered; his voice drowned out by the rain.

The armored figure thought back to a few minutes before, recalling what had happened. Two people had ambushed him, a wolf-therian and a hybrid fox-therian with three tails. The attack had triggered some protocol inside, which had resulted in the armored form he was now in, the same armored form that was in his dream. He had defended himself by generating a large amount of electricity from his body, like in the dream, and fleeing while they were distracted.

I transformed again, he thought to himself as his body relaxed, thinking he had lost them. Is it triggered by danger? No, I've been in danger before. Maybe not quite like this, but... He looked around as he continued to contemplate the matter. Something's different.

An unexpected sonic boom knocked him right off his feet. He could feel shockwaves throughout his body from the incredible sound. He landed on his back, too shocked, and disoriented to get up right away. Then a high-heeled boot found its way onto his chest.

"Who are you and what do you want?" he managed to get out as he lifted his head to see who it was. It was the three-tailed fox-therian who was leaning over him, with blue fox ears, three blue fox tails, and caramel skin. The sense of recognition was overwhelming.

"Oh, don't be that way, Marcus," she replied in a sultry voice, the grin on her face exposing sharp canines. The soft demeanor he was used to was replaced by a sinister one.

"It can't be," he uttered, his voice full of disbelief. "A... Azura?"

"In the flesh," she confirmed, removing her boot from his chest, and taking a step back.

"But," he started. "Why? What's going on? Why did you attack me? And who was that with you?" It was too much to comprehend all at once. "And... how are you a therian when you looked human before?" Being attacked by therians was one thing, but Azura being one of them? It was like he was in a dream; no, a nightmare!

"I could be asking you questions as well," she countered. "Like why do you have that armor? Why were you dreaming of slaughtering therians, Chimera like me? Do you even know?"

"Chimera?!" he burst in an accusatory tone through gritted teeth. "You're one of those animals?! Why date me when you're one of them? They hate androids! And why hide what you are in the first place?" Marcus's shock faded away, replaced by anger and the sting of betrayal.

"You don't have a clue, do you, "dear"? What better way to get close to someone and make them let their guard down?" she taunted. "As for hiding what I am, would you have trusted me if you knew I was the enemy?" Then the fox-therian bent over, getting in his face. "Satisfied?" she asked with a toothy grin.

"Hardly," Marcus grumbled. How could he be satisfied with the revelation that his girlfriend was associated with the enemy of earth and had only pretended to care about him this entire time? I should've known better than to think that such a beautiful woman would go out with an android. Even one as human as me. He felt like a great fool.

Azura stood back up, the wolf-therian from earlier showing up behind her. He wore a pleased smirk, showing off his fangs, like he had just cornered an elk and was about to feast. This one appeared like a regular therian, fully covered in brown fur and sporting wolf ears and a tail.

"Name's Randor, head of the Chimera Elite," he introduced himself nonchalantly as if he hadn't just attacked Marcus only a few minutes earlier. Then, just as suddenly as he appeared, he snatched Marcus by the neck and held him up at arm's length. "And heir of the Chimera Regime!" he boomed, purposefully deepening his voice.

A little theatrical, Marcus thought as he glared at him and snarled. He raised his own arm and unleashed an immense blast of electricity that knocked Randor off his feet.

"You?" Marcus mocked. "Don't make me laugh!" There was no way the Chimera Empire's heir would be on earth, let alone taking an interest in him. This had to be just some punk with delusions of grandeur.

Randor had landed on his face. He struggled to get up, claws digging into the pavement. His eyes showed the pain he was in and the rage of being taken off guard so easily.

"Randor!" Azura exclaimed, leaping toward Marcus immediately and unleashing a fury of emerald flames from her hand. He instinctively threw his arms up in front of his face, an electromagnetic shield forming in front of him.

Another sonic boom came and knocked Marcus off his feet, this time slamming him into the wall of a building. It cracked from the force of the impact, pieces falling to the ground. Marcus fell, landing on his hands and knees. He was even more irritated now. The sonic booms, which he had figured came from Randor somehow, were messing with his systems and made it hard to reorient himself.

When his hearing righted itself, he could hear sirens approaching fast. "Freeze!" someone shouted. "What's going on here?!"

Thinking quickly, Marcus deactivated his armored form, reverting to his normal human-like appearance. This was not something he wanted to explain to the police, especially considering he didn't have an explanation whatsoever. Even though he could see his brother among them, it still would likely be a hassle and he had dealt with enough already.

Both Randor and Azura turned, now in a panic that three police androids had arrived. One of the androids warned, "Freeze!" once again, his arm having turned into a cannon and was at the ready to fire. Azura hastily unleashed a flurry of flames, engulfing the androids. Randor leaped forward as the flames dissipated, jabbing a knife into the android's arm cannon.

"We don't have to deal with those tin heads!" Azura's voice came from the roof of a nearby building. There was an eerie, glowing purple disk behind her. Marcus hadn't a clue what it was, nor had he even noticed Azura escaping the fray.

"I agree!" Randor concurred as he jumped onto the fire escape ladder that Azura appeared to have used. Plasma blasts hit the wall near him as he scrambled up. Azura had already disappeared into the purple disk, Randor leaped into it as he arrived at the top. In seconds, the disk shrank and disappeared in a flash.

"Are you okay, Marcus?" one of the officers asked as he grabbed Marcus' hand to help him up.

"Yeah, and what about you?" he asked his brother.

"This?" he questioned, pointing to the long cut on his cannon. "It's just a scratch."

Marcus gestured to a cut on his arm, just below the shoulder; he had gotten it right before he transformed. "What I got is "just a scratch". You might need repairs."

"Eh, maybe later," his brother dismissed, switching his cannon back into an arm.

Marcus crossed his arms and smirked. "And Mom is always worried about me."

There's a reason for that, his brother thought as he turned and started walking away. He seemed distant for some reason. "My shift ends soon. You can ride with me."

"If you insist." Marcus felt that it would be nice to not have to walk home after what had just happened. With that strange portal, they could reappear at any time at any place. Could the police even catch them?

Shortly, Marcus and his brother were on one of the police maglev cycles cruising down the road on the way home. Marcus was silent for a while, but then decided to speak up. "What if I... spontaneously found a battle mode?" he posed. "Hypothetically."

"I don't know...? I have one, you know. It wouldn't be that odd." His brother seemed focused and overly tense.

"You were built for battle. I wasn't." Marcus pointed out.

"I don't know," he repeated. "Maybe it'd be a "just in case"."

"Then why wouldn't I be told?" Marcus asked, the hypothetical part of his question seemingly forgotten.

"How should I know? Look, just don't worry about it!" His brother knew there was nothing hypothetical about this. Marcus was not one to be subtle about anything. "As long as you keep it a secret, you'll be fine!"

Marcus looked down, unsatisfied with the answer. They rode the rest of the way in silence. Neither wanted to continue the conversation or face what it may mean.

When they arrived home, Marcus just went off to his room after depositing his shoes in a rack in the entrance room. He stared at the floor on the way there, deep in thought. I don't know about keeping this secret. What if I transform in public and people see it's me? They'll probably think I'm dangerous and unstable, especially if they know it's as much of a mystery to me as it is to them. This is actually happening, right? The pain sure feels real...

He sat down at his desk and opened his laptop. I'll just let my arm heal. It doesn't hurt that much. I'd rather not deal with Mom right now. He logged in and opened a messaging app. I wonder if Zeke is on.

He typed, "you on?" into the text box and hit enter.

"yep! what's up?" came in reply.

Marcus typed, "you will not believe the night I had" and sent it.

CHAPTER 2

The Mecha City Tech Convention was
crowded, as all conventions were. Marcus
could hear the hustle and bustle of the
people, as noisy as a hive full of bees and
about as unpleasant, except there wasn't
the tantalizing reward of honey to be found.
He still needed time to think about what

had happened the night before but there was no way to be alone with his thoughts in a place such as this.

Even so, his thoughts persistently wandered back to what had happened, unable to focus on anything else. He had once again transformed into that mysterious armor. For what purpose did he have a battle mode? He wasn't a soldier or a police officer like Nova. His armor didn't even look like either one, being a custom design.

Then there were the therians who had attacked him. What was it that they wanted from him? Azura being one of them was even more puzzling. She had pretended to be his girlfriend this entire time, had pretended to care about him. What did she plan to gain from that? Was it just to toy with him? If she worked for a company that rivaled his mother's, then he would understand, however, she was with a therian who claimed to be the heir of the Chimera Regime. If he truly was what he claimed to be, what was he doing all the way here on earth and why was he so interested in a simple android? Was it connected to his armor somehow? Was it related to the dream he had of fighting Chimera on Mars? There had to be some connection. There was no other explanation he could think of.

He was torn from his thoughts by a hand plopping down on his shoulder. He looked back to see his mother: the famous Masumi Valko, prominent in the field of robotics. In fact, she was probably the best programmer, A.I. or otherwise, in the country, if not the world. She had also built Marcus, the first and still only, techno-organic android in the world. People in the tech world and beyond still speculated as to how she did it, considering her husband—the engineer behind the Valroids, or Valko androids—had been dead for twenty years prior to Marcus' activation and reveal.

"How's your arm, Marcus?" she inquired, her voice sounding nonchalant and not betraying any hint of concern. She didn't want to admit just how serious this was or give the reporters something to gossip about. It had been enough just to keep what happened last night quiet, the perks of having an android son on the force, not that Nova ever enjoyed using his power to pull strings for the family. Such was already the gossip of the news stations and magazines, though Nova had proved his loyalty to his duty as a police officer time and time again.

Marcus didn't respond, feeling as if his mouth was sealed shut. It would be just another dismissive "fine" anyway, just as the other times he was asked. Why would it have changed now? For that matter, why did he have to be at this convention anyway? It's not like he was on display, as Azura had pointed out, like the various bionics or lesser robots produced by Valko Industries. It was just a waste of time to him.

He decided he needed to be alone, or as alone as one could be in a crowd of noisy people, heading in the direction of the food court. A female android with violet hair and skin like that of a porcelain doll—his sister, Nebula—noticed him leaving and watched with a look of concern. He had been assaulted by some extremely dangerous people and she was wondering how he was handling it. Sometimes he was hard to read, tending to mask his emotions and act like he was fine when he was not, but he was clearly distressed. It could just be the crowd, but she highly doubted that was all it was.

Marcus navigated through the crowd and found the end of a line. It was short, thankfully. When it was his turn, he ordered a soft pretzel with cheese. He paid the cashier, took his food, and selected a seat in an empty booth as far away from other people as possible. He sat down his food, pulling the lid off the container of piping hot melted cheese. He tore off a piece of pretzel and dipped it into the cheese, but he didn't raise it to his mouth to take a bite; instead, he only continued poking at the cheese. His legs kicked back and forth.

He was made aware of the outside world yet again when someone came over, planting his hands on the table. The left one was bionic, appearing like the arm of an android, similar in design to Marcus' own arms. The other arm was fully human as was its owner.

"Hey, Marcus! How's it going?" the newcomer asked, a wide smile on his face that just radiated energy, a stark contrast to Marcus' gloomy disposition.

Marcus was silent at first, continuing to poke at his cheese. "The Chimera Elite are bothering me, Zeke," he finally replied.

"Worrying about those losers won't change a thing, ya know," Zeke pointed out as he sat down, bionic arm resting on the table.

"Knowing that won't help me worry less," Marcus stated. The one had claimed to be the heir of the Chimera Regime, after all. He wasn't just some random punk picking a fight if he was telling the truth. He had a reason for attacking him. What was it? Why had he only attacked now? They had been keeping an eye on him for a while now. It was unnerving not to know why.

"Well, sure, but..." It wasn't easy for Zeke to argue with that. Anxiety wasn't something one could just negotiate with or reason away. "Just try to get your mind off it. Ya wouldn't want them to be happy you're down in the dumps, right?"

Marcus looked over at the Valko Industries booth, not really interested in what Zeke had to say, only to see it burst into flames. He traced the fire to the hands of a mysterious figure, who had fox ears and a fox tail. Azura wasn't the only fox-therian with pyrokinesis.

"Rubi?" he whispered, dropping his pretzel. He shot up out of his seat and sped towards her, leaving Zeke confused and full of questions.

Back at the booth, Rubi stood before Nova, a wall of flames behind her. Her eyes had a blank gaze as she stared him down. Nova raised his arm cannon, ordering for her to stand down. She held out her arm and snapped her fingers, a jet of flame bursting forth and surrounding Nova. He put his arms up to shield his face.

Rubi twisted her body as she swung a kick that landed squarely on Nova's midsection, knocking him over. Two other android police officers stepped beside him on either side. One fired his arm cannon, but Rubi dodged the blast. She evaded the lasers several times more as she charged ahead. She leapt into the air and kicked an arm cannon that was about to fire. The laser accidentally hit the other officer.

Nova got back up and attempted to subdue her. As he approached, her right hand became covered in a glove of flames. When he was close enough, she plunged her burning hot hand into his chest, melting through the armor. Her claws dug into the android's core. Pain shot throughout his chest as the core was ripped out, wires tearing and snapping. The pain stopped, and his lifeless body hit the floor.

Marcus stared wide-eyed at the sight before him. A pain spread throughout his body like a frost. He could not move, could not act; he couldn't think. He just stared at his brother's core-less body. Anger arose, slowly beginning to burn through the frost. Masumi stared on in horror.

Marcus finally broke out of his stupor. Anger burned inside him, initiating a program; he could feel himself start to transform. Nanites began forming over his chest, a blue triangle with a smaller black triangle inside, red surrounding it. The nanites spread upward, downward, and outward until his whole body was covered in armor of red, black and gold. He wasn't afraid this time.

He lunged forward, slugging the fox-therian. Her head turned away from the impact and she fell to the ground. Marcus came at her again, building up electricity in his hands. He leaped forward, aiming a punch at her. Before it hit, she rolled out of the way, his fist contacting the floor instead.

"Why are you doing this?" he asked, eyes wide in rage.

Rubi sent a jet of flame in his direction. He brought up an electromagnetic shield in front of him to block the fire. When the fire dissipated, he took the electricity of the shield and formed it into a ball between his hands. He unleashed it on Rubi, the shock causing her steps to falter.

Where Nova had fallen, Masumi knelt beside him. She kept looking back and forth between Nova's body and the battling android. It would be no easy task to lift Nova. He was an android in full police armor, which was far heavier than the average human. Masumi managed to get one of the remaining police androids to carry him out, only carrying the core herself. They were staying clear of the battle, only focusing on getting people to safety now since it was obvious that they were outclassed.

What we are we going to do? Masumi asked herself.

A barrage of fireballs launched at Marcus, who quickly moved to dodge. He couldn't evade all of them, but the fire didn't faze him; he was too focused on the battle to care. Marcus leaped forward and pinned her to the wall.

"Why did you attack?! Why did you kill Nova?!" he demanded while giving her low-level shocks repeatedly after each question in an attempt to force a response. "Were you just a spy too?! Why?! What do you people want from me?!"

Not getting anywhere, Marcus just tossed her aside. She skidded across the floor, people quickly moving out of the way. Among them was Zeke and his father, who were walking along the wall to escape the room.

Marcus jumped in front of the people to shield them from Rubi. She got up from the floor quickly and charged at him. She leapt into the air, flipping over, and landing a foot on his chest. He lost his footing and fell backward, squishing someone against the wall. He quickly dashed off to take a swing at Rubi who dodged his fist.

"Zeke!" a man cried in a whisper tone. His son had slid down the wall and appeared half-conscious. The main glared over at the two battlers, and then looked back to his son. He noticed a piece of red metal on the ground. He picked it up, looking again at the android. The point of his top helmet spike was missing. He quickly put the piece in his pocket and picked up Zeke, making his way to the exit.

I've got to stop her! Marcus thought as he generated electricity around his hands. The blue lights on his chest, wrists, and belt were all glowing bright, the charge building up in his body. He moved in quickly, grabbing Rubi by the sides of her head and unleashing as much electricity as he could. She was silent at first, but then the blank stare left her eyes and she screamed. Then her eyes closed, and her body went limp.

Somewhere in the crowd, another scream was heard, and a hooded figure collapsed. Someone went to check on the person, pulling the hood back to find that she was a lynx-therian. A police officer directed some EMTs to take her.

"Rubi?" Marcus whispered. He could tell that she was still breathing but she wasn't moving otherwise.

Marcus just stood there as a police officer took Rubi off his hands; his arms stayed up like he was still holding her, and he stared off into space. A lot had just happened in a short span of time and he wasn't sure what to do now. Why did Rubi attack? He hadn't thought she was one of them. Had he been tricked again?

"Who are you?" one of the police officers asked, breaking him from his trance.

Marcus didn't answer at first, trying to think of what he should say. Somehow, he didn't think giving his real name was a good idea. He didn't want people knowing it was he who had this armor. Finally, he replied, "Dynamo."

The police officers put Rubi in restraints and took her from the convention center. Marcus wanted to follow but knew that wasn't a good idea. There was nothing he could do at this point and it would just make the police more suspicious about his connection to her.

Why had he given that name and where did it come from? He knew what a dynamo was; it was an electrical generator. Was that why he picked it? No, his head had been nowhere near clear enough to think of something as clever as that. It had come to him from somewhere in the back of his mind. It was a subconscious selection. Why though?

That was a question for later. For now, he had to get out of this room. If it was overwhelming earlier, it was unbearable now. The noise level was much louder now that they all had something exciting to talk about.

He slipped through the convention center doors and stepped into the hall, shutting the door behind him. He leaned against the wall by the door and slid down, wrapping his arms around his knees, and burying his head in his lap.

Why did Rubi attack? What's up with this armor? And that name. Why did I think of that? What am I going to do? The questions swirled around in his mind, making it hard for him to come up with possible answers.

"Are you okay, Marcus?" a voice broke through his thoughts.

He looked up to see an android with pale skin like that of a porcelain doll and violet princess-cut hair. It was his sister, Nebula.

"How did you-?" he started to question. He did not look like his normal self, after all.

"I know my own brother," she answered.

"I- this armor- the Chimera-" Everything started trying to come out at once; his confusion over Rubi and his armor, the chimera who attacked him before, everything.

"You don't have to explain anything," she said, crouching down to his level.

Marcus was rocking back and forth at this point, eyes shut, having given up trying to talk. He could explain later if he wanted to. He'd have to tell them about the armor, how it came to him the night before, eventually. He wasn't sure about telling them about anything else, about telling them about Rubi.

Before Marcus knew it, he could feel his consciousness slipping away and his body slowly falling to the floor.

"Marcus? Marcus!" his sister shouted.

Nebula crouching over him was the last thing he saw before everything went black.

CHAPTER 3

When Marcus came to, he was on a repair chair in a white room. It was fully reclined, flat as a table except for the spot under his head, which had extra cushioning. He was strapped down, only in his pants and socks.

Did he pass out? He didn't remember doing so, but everything was a blur after defeating Rubi. In fact, much of what happened before that was a blur as well. He remembered enough to know what had happened, but it wasn't perfectly clear, like trying to see through a fog. Some parts were clearer, like what had happened to Nova, but the details of the fight were not. It felt like a faded dream.

He looked around to see if anyone was still there. He'd rather not stay strapped to the chair. Why was he strapped down anyway? He noticed that he was in the laboratory tucked away in the basement of the Valko mansion, seeing the wall of computer terminals and the huge monitors mounted on the wall. That meant he was home.

"Hello?" he called out weakly. He hoped someone was there. The restraints were becoming uncomfortable. Not only did they physically keep him in place, but they emitted a magnetic field to prevent him from moving around too much. Most extensive repairs were done when the android was offline but, as a techno-organic android, Marcus couldn't be brought offline. This made the restraints a must as he could jerk and damage himself or hurt whoever was repairing him. Still, he hadn't recalled taking any serious damage and so was still puzzled.

"I see you're awake," a voice said, the sound footsteps approaching.

"Did I... pass out?" he questioned.

"Yes, you did." The voice's owner, Masumi, checked something on a holographic screen separate from the monitors. Then she walked over and began undoing the straps.

"Why?" Marcus sat up as soon as he could, flexing his arms and fingers.

"Overload," Masumi replied. "Your systems were overtaxed. Most likely because of everything that happened earlier."

Marcus nodded, processing his mother's answer. Maybe his systems weren't used to handling that kind of power and that was actually why. Yet, that power seemed somewhat familiar, like he had been used to it before some time ago; like seeing an old place long forgotten. It was a terribly strong déjà vu.

"Where is everyone?" he asked, sliding off the chair.

"Nova's over there." Masumi pointed to another fully reclined repair chair across the room where Nova's lifeless body lied. He had been manually shifted out of his police armor and was also strapped down. His chest still had a gaping hole in it where his power core was ripped out. "Nebula returned to work. I don't know where Zeke went."

"Can he be fixed?" Marcus asked.

"Probably," she replied. "I've been working on his wiring. I just have to reinstall his core and plug him in. Repair systems should do the rest. Nanites really are convenient." She paused. "The only problem is the sudden loss of power to his systems. There could be some damage to his coding which I may not be able to fix. Probably nothing major, but…"

"Still not a good thing," Marcus finished for her. Code damage was a serious problem for an android, depending on how extensive or what part of their coding it was. Even if the android could function, other problems could arise. Common problems were existential crises or identity confusion, which often led to madness. Sometimes it was benign, other times, the android would become violent. People were usually very wary of androids with severely damaged code, especially if it was in the behavior sector. It brought up humanity's old fears of a robot rebellion from their media two centuries ago.

"No." Masumi resumed her work on Nova, checking wires to see if they needed to be replaced. It seemed as though she was purposefully avoiding any further conversation.

"Um, I'm going to head up to my room now for a bit. I'm good to go, right?" he asked, still not sure what needed to be repaired in the first place. Did he switch out of his armor before his mother got to him or had he been forced out of it like Nova? Did Nebula mention the armor?

"Everything checks out. You should be fine so long as nothing exciting happens," Masumi replied.

"Yeah, okay." Not that he could make any promises. None of the excitement had been of his choosing.

"Jyaa mata," she dismissed as Marcus went to leave. He walked over to and entered the small elevator across the room and pushed the button for the second floor. The door closed and the cylinder carried him up two floors. He stepped out and went to the left, entering the first door he came to.

Once in his room, Marcus made his way over to his bed and flopped down. A hamster scurried over and crawled up his bed sheets to him. It was cream-colored and had a white band around its middle. It crawled up next to his face.

"Got out again, huh?" Marcus turned his head toward the hamster. "What am I going to do with you?" he asked, then sighed, "What am I going to do?" His hamster only stared at him.

He could've easily asked his mother about this, but something kept him from doing so as if he was physically unable to ask even though he was able to speak of other things. Was it even possible that his mother didn't know? Could this be something Dr. Valko did before he died? The man was responsible for the mechanical side of Valroids. He had been killed twenty years ago by Chimera, long before Marcus was activated, but it did take some time to construct an android as advanced as he was. How long had he been in production? Was it long enough for Dr. Valko to be able add a battle mode without his mother's knowledge? No, a master programmer like her wouldn't have missed something like that. So why was she avoiding addressing the issue? The elephant wasn't going to leave the room just because it was ignored.

More concerning still was the Chimera Elite. They were bad news and that was a colossal understatement as they were supposed to be a kind of special forces. What did they want with him? Sure, the Chimera tended to hate androids and robots in general. They were the reason the Chimera had lost the war and failed to conquer the earth. Therians were stronger than humans, but robots were even stronger than them. Even so, Marcus doubted it was as simple as that as they would've just taken him out months ago. No, there was something more to this.

Then there was Rubi. Could she actually be working with the other Chimera like Azura? Marcus thought back to how he had met Rubi. That had also been the first time he had discovered his armored form. It was a few months ago.

Marcus had been walking down a trail deep in the park, one of his favorite places to be alone and think. That day, his thoughts had been occupied with the possibilities of his future. He was majoring in astronomy, but he didn't know what his career should be, what he wanted to do with his degree when he got it. Marcus had only chosen it because it was one of his main passions; as for his others, they didn't offer degrees in sword collecting or playing video games. Of course, the prospect of being an astronaut had always interested him, but his fantasy of space travel from sci-fi movies, shows, books, and games had only resulted in reality being a disappointment to him. He was often lost in fantasies of exotic adventures and felt that real-life could not bring him such wonderment.

He had been pulled from his thoughts when he had heard some unusual rustling off the path. He had peered into the bushes by the path to see a fox therian. He had wondered what she was doing hiding in the park. His thoughts had gone to Nox, a bat-therian whom he had met in high school; he had often been on the receiving end of bullying and still sometimes was, even in college. He had wondered if she was hiding from someone.

"Hey, what're you doing in there?" he had asked, stepping forward.

She had backed up and growled.

"Why don't you come out of there? It's not a good idea to go off the trail." He had knelt down to get closer to her.

The therian had suddenly leaped at him. She had knocked him down, having rolled to the side and standing on all fours. She had attacked again. He had had no time to dodge or try to get away.

After having knocked him around a bit, she had pinned him against a tree. She had called flames to her hand and had plunged her searing fingers into his chest, digging her claws into his power core, just as she would do to Nova latter. He had thought it was over and he hadn't even known why she had attacked. That had been when something triggered inside him.

Starting at his chest, nanites had begun covering his entire body. It hadn't been long before he was decked in shiny metal armor from head to toe. He had been in shock, having momentarily forgotten the pain in his chest and the danger he had been in; but not for long as he had instinctively generated electricity from his chest. She had fallen backward and had hit the ground.

He had put a hand to his throbbing chest and had stood over the therian. She had gotten up but only to all fours like a wild beast, hanging back from him. She had clearly been surprised.

"Why did you attack me?" he had asked.

The therian hadn't answered. Her body had started to shift, having taken on a more human appearance. Now the only fox traits that had remained were her ears and tail, the latter of which had been twitching.

"Wha-? How did you-?" He had never seen a therian do that before. They weren't supposed to be shapeshifters. In fact, he had never heard of any organic shapeshifters. Only some robots had that capability, and it was usually limited. He, apparently, was one of those robots as evidenced by the armor covering his body.

She had then stood up on two legs that time and had slowly walked over to him. He had tensed; having been nervous that she would attack again. She had hesitantly raised her hand, having placed it on his hand, which had still been covering his chest.

"What?" He hadn't known what she had been trying to say to him. She wasn't acting hostile anymore, but he couldn't just assume she wasn't going to attack again.

The fox-therian's ears had drooped to the side and she had looked incredibly sad. Somehow, he had gotten the impression that she was trying to apologize. If she had regretted attacking him, why had she done it in the first place? He hadn't understood it at all. Even now, he didn't understand her actions. Her behavior toward him had shifted between two extremes in an extremely short span of time without any real indicator as to why. He supposed his armor had something to do with it, but he still couldn't fathom why.

She had removed her hand, clasping both just in front of her chest. She had tilted her head to the side and had lifted her ears up, twitching them.

"I still don't know what you're trying to tell me." He had suddenly got an idea and had reached for his phone, only to be reminded of the armor that had been covering his body at the time. "Arg! Where did this armor even come from?"

She had given a confused look, her ears twitching again. It seemed to be her indicator of curiosity.

"Yes, that's right. This is the first time this's happened. Don't suppose you have anything to do with it?" he had asked, having highly doubting that possibility. It was an incredibly absurd idea, though he had been mostly joking. On the other hand, he would have never guessed that a therian could shapeshift or generate fire. With all the other therian abilities he would encounter afterward, it didn't seem quite so absurd anymore. Nothing really did.

She had closed her eyes and had shaken her head in response.

"That's what I thought." Marcus had closed his eyes and had attempted to focus in an attempt to make the armor disappear. He had wondered how Nova did it. He had become silent, his artificial lungs taking even breaths. As a techno-organic android, he needed to breathe as much as humans did.

The nanites had retreated the way they had come, having left him in his original form. His shirt had had holes in it from the therian's attack, but his clothes had been intact otherwise. He had pulled his phone out of his cargo pants pocket, being surprised to find it undamaged. He had typed in his code to unlock it and had pulled up an app. He had handed the phone to her. "Here."

She had taken the phone and had analyzed the screen for a few moments to understand what he had wanted her to do. She had begun typing and then had touched an on-screen button. The device had spoken, saying, "Will you be okay?"

"I don't know. Probably? I'm still standing," he had answered, shrugging. "Doesn't seem like you hit anything critical. It just hurts. Self-repair will probably kick in."

"Sorry," the device had said.

"Why'd you attack me in the first place?" Marcus had asked again, having wondered if he would ever get an answer. "I wasn't even doing anything. Just walking by."

The therian had looked away. "I have to go now," the device had spoken. She had handed his phone back and had turned around, having shifted back into full therian form.

"Wait!" he had called out, but it had been too late. She had already disappeared into the trees. After a few moments, he had looked back to his chest. He had zipped up his jacket, having decided to stay away from home for a little while until it had healed.

Marcus' thoughts returned to the current situation. Had Rubi been meant to attack him all along? Was she working with the other Chimera? If so, why did she stop and apologize? Did she have a reluctant part in this? He had to find out. Not just for his own curiosity, but to help this troubled girl. Azura had used him and he didn't like the prospect of the Elite using Rubi as well.

CHAPTER 4

A soft knock came at Marcus' door, which then opened to reveal his mother. "Marcus, I got a call from Dr. Gates about the two therians taken to the hospital. He says he found something interesting. Want to come?"

Marcus simply nodded.

"Okay, honey." His mother left, closing the door gently.

He got up and put his hamster back in its cage. Then he picked out a shirt to put on, having yet to redress, and threw a jacket over it. Marcus left his room, walking down the large stairs that led to the entrance room; there was a wraparound staircase on either side of the elevator in case of power outages. He left through the front door, only to notice a crowd of people at the front gate. Dealing with nosy reporters was an unfortunate and inevitable part of his life, being experimental new technology built by the owner of one of the best technology companies in the world, and he hated it. He gathered up his courage, walking to the garage. He knew they were talking, asking questions, but his ears did not register their words. He simply entered the garage and got in the car, not making any eye contact.

Masumi was already in the car, not looking any happier about the reporters at her door, mumbling something about building a robot guard dog that would shoot lasers from its eyes. They were silent as she drove out of the garage, down the drive past the reporters and onto the road. It wasn't long before they arrived at the hospital.

They were escorted to the hospital room where Rubi and the mysterious lynx-therian were being kept. The two were in beds next to each other, both unconscious and with electrodes attached to their foreheads.

"So, what's so interesting that you called me here?" Masumi asked, skipping past the pleasantries, as always.

Dr. Gates turned from his monitor and faced the two, unfazed by Masumi jumping to the point. "Ah, yes. The readings I found analyzing the cat girl's brainwaves. They're very... unusual. Look at them for yourself." He gestured to the monitor, which displayed the brainwaves of both therians side-by-side.

Masumi stepped forward; she had studied neurology to further improve her AI programming and so was familiar with it. "This... cannot be."

"What can't be?" Marcus asked, raising a brow, and looking over her shoulder at the readings, not that he'd have a clue what they meant.

She shook her head. "These readings... They seem to indicate... telepathy."

"What?" Marcus was taken aback, but Dr. Gates seemed nonplussed. It was an incredulous claim, even after encountering shapeshifting, pyrokinesis, and some sonic scream ability.

"Telepathy," she repeated. "Her brain can send signals into other people's brains, almost like WIFI." It was an oversimplification, but she did not feel like delving into all the theories or terminology. She scrolled through the readouts. "I assume these readings are from the fox-therian?"

"Yes, they are," Gates confirmed. "They indicate that her brain was affected by an outside force, presumably the cat girl. Their two nervous systems were connected, linked by this WIFI connection as you call it, which would explain why the cat girl collapsed when the fox girl was electrocuted."

"So, it wasn't her fault?" Marcus questioned. They were silent, surprised by his question. "It wasn't her fault she killed Nova. She was forced to attack." A pause. "Right?"

"That does appear to be the case," Gates confirmed. "Her readings also indicated that she was in something of a deep sleep like her consciousness was turned off while the cat girl was controlling her."

Marcus nodded. The information eased his mind. Rubi wasn't another traitor. It was a relief, even though he had spent much less time with Rubi than he had with Azura. He wished to go stand by her bedside and comfort her even though she wasn't awake, but he didn't want anyone finding out that he knew her. Not yet.

He was pulled from his thoughts when he noticed the others starting to leave the room. Taking a last glance at Rubi and vowing to return sometime to talk to her, he followed the group. No sooner did they start to pass through the door did they hear... some strange sound like the fabric of space being torn, if one could imagine how that would sound. They turned to see a five-foot circular disc with a purple hue, which Marcus recognized from that night. A green boot stepped out of the portal, followed by the rest of Randor's body. He let out a sonic scream, clearing the three out of the room and slamming them into the adjacent wall. The police androids stationed to guard the entrance quickly ran into the room to deal with the invader. While the others were picking themselves up, Marcus slipped off down the hall. He rounded the corner and double-checked that he was alone. Satisfied that there was no one to see him, he closed his eyes and transformed into his armor. After taking a focused breath, he took off back down the hall towards the room.

Marcus jumped back as a police android flew into the hallway and hit the wall. After a few moments of shock, he walked over to see if the android was alright. Marcus shook him but there was no response. He turned to look through the doorway. He could see Randor and now Azura battling against the police.

Marcus charged into the room, ready to take them on again. Not paying attention to the floor, he tripped over another android's body. Randor's attention shifted, looking at the newcomer from the corner of his eye. The corner of his mouth curved up and he turned to face him.

"Ha! Ha-ha-ha! This is your great hero?!He can't even stay on his feet!" Randor mocked.

Marcus got up, getting into a defensive stance. "Leave them alone! Now!" he barked, ignoring the insult and shoving the embarrassment of such a foolish mistake to the back of his mind.

"You and what army will stop me? The guards are broken, and you're outnumbered." Randor stepped closer, fingers curled inward to show off his claws.

"Didn't you learn anything from the war? Robots are stronger than therians," Marcus pointed out, despite the fallen guards. They were police-grade, not military grade.

"Oh, we learned." Randor lashed out, clawing at Marcus's face. "And we've improved." He slashed at Marcus again. "We've gotten stronger."

Marcus could feel cuts in his helmet, having ducked in time to avoid damage to his face. How are therian claws able to do that?! They should be breaking on contact or at least glancing off! What experiments could they be doing to result in this?

Marcus lunged forward to tackle Randor, forcing him to the ground and pinning his arms to the floor. Randor bit Marcus' neck, his teeth making holes in his armor. Marcus held position, hoping he couldn't do any serious damage, still mind boggled that it was even possible for his teeth to pierce metal.

Meanwhile, Azura was busy removing the IVs and electrodes from Rubi. She had already done the same to Neva, who she had unceremoniously tossed through the portal. Rubi began to stir, repeatedly blinking to try to keep her eyes open. She was not yet fully aware of her surroundings, only seeing vague shapes of different colors.

"I told Randor that using you was a bad idea. You can't succeed if your heart's not in the job. Mind-control isn't enough. Especially for someone as stubborn as you."

That voice brought her to reality. Rubi quickly shot up to a sitting position and scooted back on the bed, getting into a defensive position, and snarling. She couldn't just scare Azura off with her flames since she was also a pyrokinetic; it'd have zero effect on her. She waited, hoping Azura would get closer.

"You're useless. I don't know why Randor keeps you around at all. You've been more trouble than you're worth. And associating with a machine? Some Chimera you are."

Azura's contempt for androids was not hidden.

Rubi lunged at Azura, knocking her on her back. Rubi jumped up and dashed to the window, hastily flinging it open. She slipped out and fell down the side of the building quite a few floors. She landed amongst a row of bushes in a patch of mulch. After a few moments of stillness, she rose and hobbled out. Rubi quickly limped away.

Azura leaned on the windowsill, scowling at her escaped prisoner. So much for showing up Neva. She had just failed at the same task. Or perhaps not. She could still chase after her. Rubi wouldn't be very fast in this state.

Several police androids arrived in the room, aiming their blasters at Azura.

"Freeze!" the foremost one yelled. "You're under arrest!"

Azura grinned before whipping around and blasting them all with a great burst of green flames. They screamed and shortly collapsed, their silicone skin and metal armor melting. The fox was satisfied in taking her frustrations out on the androids. Now she had to determine her next move.

Marcus hit the wall back-first. He ducked down just as Randor's claws raked across the wall. He lunged forward, sending an uppercut right into the wolf-therian's stomach. He hit the ground hard, hugging his abdomen and coughing up blood.

Azura turned to assess Randor's situation. It seemed the great prince wasn't doing so well. She dashed over, sending a kick flying at Marcus. He blocked with an arm and sent her across the room with a push.

Randor stood up, backing away from Marcus, clawed hands guarding his midsection. Fighting him here and now hadn't exactly been in the plan and continuing wouldn't further his goal. Marcus wasn't ready for them to really do battle. Not yet.

"Azura..." Randor continued to back up as Marcus followed him, electricity dancing around the android's hand. "I think it's time we left."

"Yes, Randor." Azura didn't waste any time diving through the portal. Randor wasn't far behind her, tripping up Marcus on his way out.

"Get back here!" Marcus lunged forward to pursue them, but the portal disappeared. He fell flat on the ground. Marcus decided to just lie there, not feeling like moving right away. There were no more threats and nothing more he could do.

After a few moments, Masumi crept into the room and over to him. She knelt beside Marcus and placed a hand on his back.

"Are you... okay?" It had been quite the battle; one she had not been used to for a long time.

Marcus forced himself to his knees. "Yeah... Yes, I'm fine. I'm fine..." He wondered if she knew it was him. She had to by now if she hadn't already known.

Gates stepped over cautiously, studying Marcus with a suspicious gaze. "Who are you? Where did you come from? Why do you keep showing up around us?"

They were the questions Marcus knew would come. He didn't know how he should answer or if he should keep the secret from him if it even was a secret at this point.

Surely, Gates realized that "Marcus" was the only one not present.

"I..." He was at a loss of what to say. He wanted to keep the secret, but he just couldn't bring himself to lie. He went to fall sideways, his mother catching him. He was just so tired, so worn out. Not from physical exhaustion. He could go all day so long as he had a decent charge. There was just so much to sort through, to figure out.

"It's okay," she said in a soothing voice. "It'll be okay."

Gates looked at them both but kept quiet. It didn't look like he'd be getting his answers. He wondered just how long he would be in the dark. Masumi knew something, he was sure. For that matter, where was Marcus?

CHAPTER 5

Marcus was in the basement laboratory
of the Valko mansion. Masumi had been
working on Nova for some time, connecting
his wires to a brand-new core, but she
wasn't there currently. It took time for the
rest of his body's nanites to accept the
nanites of the new core and for that core to

charge, a process that she didn't need to be present for.

To busy himself while he waited, Marcus was rummaging through the lab. There were boxes that hadn't been touched in ages, evident by the copious amounts of dust covering them. He had no idea if they'd hold the answers, but he didn't know many other places to look. It couldn't hurt, in any case, and he had nothing better to do. He opened the first one and started digging through, making his way through all of them.

Inside were old parts, probably prototypes, mementos, most likely. Though, most of such things were on display in the mansion or at Valko Industries' main building. He dug deeper, pulling out a lone flash drive. Intrigued, he plugged it into the main computer.

It was encrypted, as expected. Marcus, however, knew the software Masumi used to encrypt and decrypt things. It wasn't something she had shown him. He had just seen it done before when she thought he wasn't paying attention. After a while, the drive was unlocked, and he could access the files.

They were blueprints; Valroid blueprints. He recognized Nova and Nebula's blueprints among them, which was not surprising. It was always a good idea to keep blueprints, especially of designs that advanced, and it made sense for them to be encrypted. Strangely, though, blueprints for custom armored forms like his were included. He wondered if Nova and Nebula were aware of them, or in the dark like he was. There was another set of blueprints for another android that he didn't recognize that was labeled V-004 MAGNETO, which would make him Marcus' younger brother. Why hadn't he met him or even know about him? Did Nova and Nebula know about this?

Then he came to what he was looking for: blueprints that matched his armor. They were labeled V-003 DYNAMO, the name he had given that day. At least that mystery was solved, but it still didn't explain why he had this armor or why it was kept a secret.

Nova stirred. He slowly booted up, eyes opening. He sat up with a start, grabbing his chest. After a moment, he looked down. Seeing it repaired, he relaxed, letting his hand fall to the chair.

Marcus was too enthralled with his discovery to notice. Nova looked over, eyes widening at what he saw on the screen. He attempted to get off the chair but fell, his systems still being in the process of booting. Marcus looked over. After a moment, he decided to go over and help Nova up.

"Did you know about Dynamo?" he asked immediately. "Mom won't tell me anything, but I found his... my blueprints on an encrypted flash drive that was in this lab. What's going on?"

"Marcus..." he started. How should he go about this? "You don't need to worry about it. Everything's fine."

"No! No, it's not fine! I was attacked in the alley, we were attacked at the expo and at the hospital, and this stupid armor has something to do with it!"

"Wait... the hospital?" His hand went back up to his chest again. "What happened?"

"The therian that ripped your core out was taken to the hospital with another therian that was found collapsed in the crowd right after I zapped the first one unconscious. Dr. Gates invited us to see what he had found out about the therians, which was that the cat had telepathy and had mind-controlled the fox," Marcus began explaining.

"Wait. Telepathy?" Nova interrupted.

"Yes, telepathy, Mom confirmed it, which means the fox is innocent." Marcus made sure to point that out. "Anyway, that's when the two therians from the other night came in through the same portal they escaped through that night and attacked us. They wanted the other therians back, but only got one of them. The fox escaped."

"Oh..." He didn't like hearing that. It sounded like Marcus getting attacked that night was just the beginning of something more.

"When was someone going to tell me this?!" Marcus burst. "It shows that you and Nebula have armored forms too."

Nova sighed. This was not what he wanted to deal with after having just come back online. "You didn't need to know. It was a secret and it's important that it stays that way."

"But why? What's so bad that it had to be a secret?"

"Don't bother about this." Nova didn't know everything that had happened since he had been offline for that time, but he could easily deduce that Marcus had somehow activated his armor in public. If he knew Marcus, it was probably sometime around or after he was attacked. How many people saw? He couldn't help but feel that this would end badly. "Just leave the past where it is. And put that flash drive back where and how you found it."

"This isn't over." Marcus reluctantly re-encrypted the data and removed the flash drive. He tucked it back away in the box it came from and returned that to its original place as well. "I'm going to get to the bottom of this."

Nova just stood silently, somber, as Marcus entered the elevator and left. Maybe he should've played dumb instead of letting Marcus know that he knew something about this. He knew that Marcus would stop at nothing until he uncovered the truth, no matter where it led him.

It was night. Marcus was searching the park for Rubi. He had doubts that she would be there or anywhere near Mecha City after what had happened, but he was short on ideas of where else to look. Plus, he had to find her before something else happened.

He was being quiet for the most part, only whispering her name. He didn't want anyone else to know he was here looking for her. There was no telling what might happen if someone else were to discover her or to find out that he had had contact with her before

"It's safe to come out. I'm not mad. I just want to figure out what's going on." He brushed aside some foliage. "Someone used you. Has it happened before?" He parted a bush. He wondered where she could be hiding. Marcus wanted to free her from these people. He hated to see others be taken advantage of like this. She was a poor pawn not even in control of her own actions. He couldn't even imagine what that was like, though he was starting to feel like a pawn at this point. But was he a pawn in the Chimera Elite's game or his mother's? She certainly wasn't leveling with him.

"How touching!" someone exclaimed.

Marcus, torn from his thoughts, whipped around toward the noise but could see no one yet.

"Do you really think we'll just let you take her?" A figure stepped out from the trees. It was Azura, her three tails swaying. Her very presence felt threatening. She seemed nothing like the person he knew before.

"What do you want with Rubi?!" Marcus demanded, shifting into a defensive position.

"You don't know?" she laughed. "Not very bright, are you? Then again, I guess your intelligence is artificial." She swung a kick at Marcus.

He transformed and generated an electro-shield, blocking her attack. "Oh, good one. How long did it take for you to come up with that little insult?" All day, he thought but didn't feel like adding more to his comeback. It was enough just to face her again.

"Like I'd waste time on you." She paced around him at a distance. Marcus turned as she did, keeping her in front of him.

"You mean like you're doing right now? Like you've done this whole time?" Marcus posed. He dodged to the right as a fireball came his way. "Do you even know what you're doing?" He dodged another ball, firing his own blast of electricity.

She leaped in the air to dodge his electric attack, flipping toward him, and coming down on him with a kick. Her foot contacted his head, knocking him over. She sent several more fireballs toward him, all hitting the ground around him. "I do and you'll know too soon enough, but by then it'll be too late."

Marcus scrambled to his feet. He was done trying to trick something out of her; she wasn't going to give up any information. He dodged a couple more blasts, feeling that she was missing on purpose just to toy with him.

Some of Azura's fire blasts hit a couple of trees, quickly catching the leaves on fire. Neither noticed right away, being too absorbed in watching each other's moves until they noticed the air growing significantly warmer and could smell smoke.

"Ah!" Marcus exclaimed as he realized. "Look what you did! You're gonna burn down the whole park!"

"Oops," she said as if she had simply spilled a glass of milk. "I guess that's my cue to go. Randor'd be upset if I defeated you anyway. See you later, automaton!" With that, she dashed off into the trees.

Marcus didn't bother to chase her. What would be the point? He looked around, seeing that the fire was quickly spreading. He had to get out of here quickly, but he couldn't just escape like that. There were undoubtedly other people in the park, even at this late hour. He took off down the trail, traveling deeper into the park, to rescue anyone who was there.

Azura exited a portal, entering a dimly lit room. Randor was leaning back in an office chair, going over information on a tablet in his hand. His ears twitched at her arrival, but he did not turn to look at her.

"He's transformed again," she reported, kneeling, and laying her ears back. She looked up, grinning. "And I set the park on fire."

"Good, good." He still didn't look at her. "If my theory's right, the more he transforms, the better. Toy with him as much as you like. Just remember that he's my prey."

"Of course, Randor." Azura stood up. "But why not destroy him now while he's weak? You already know it's him."

"No, not yet," Randor finally turned his gaze upon her. "He needs to remember first. I won't be satisfied with his defeat until then."

"Very well; if that's what you wish," she conceded.

"It is." Randor stood up. "It won't be a true victory until Dynamo is at full power. Battle androids were built to be stronger than therians, but I was engineered to be stronger than battle androids. I cannot truly test my strength otherwise."

Azura quietly took a deep breath. "If he's not at full power... and you're made to be stronger than battle androids... then why did it seem like he had you on the ropes in the alley and at the hospital?" She had attempted to sound neutral but there was an obvious tone of dissent in her voice.

Randor snarled, clawed fingers curling in tension. "Simple," he hissed. "If I attacked full force, I would defeat Dynamo too quickly. He'd never have the opportunity to regain his full power then, so I have to hold back." Randor turned away from Azura, folding his arms across his chest. "I just... underestimated his current power level. Which... actually works in my favor because now Dynamo will be overconfident and

underestimate my threat level. A mistake—"
He looked over his shoulder at Azura. "I
don't recommend you making."

"Yes, sir." Azura turned and left the room,
no longer wanting to have this discussion.
She needed to be more careful about what
she said to the heir of the Chimera Regime.
He may not be quite as ruthless as his
father, but he was temperamental,
especially concerning his pride as the most
powerful therian.

CHAPTER 6

The next day, Marcus and Zeke were
making their way through downtown
Mecha City, which was filled with shops and
restaurants. Benches and trees were quite
plentiful along the sidewalks, along with the
occasional trash can. Cars hovered by at a
moderate speed and other people were

traversing the sidewalks. A few basal robots puttered along, picking up trash and making sure the landscape was properly maintained.

Both were enjoying milkshakes from the local ice cream parlor and trying to forget the events of the past few days.

"I really don't know what I'm going to do," Marcus groaned as he had been doing on and off for the past few hours.

Zeke sighed, not quite annoyed, but certainly getting tired of it. "I heard ya the first hundred times, mate. I don't know what to tell ya. I got no more answers than the last time ya asked."

"I know," Marcus continued to groan. "I just... I don't like not knowing what to do or what's going on."

"You should loosen up and relax," Zeke suggested. "The world's full of endless possibilities of adventure. Just enjoy the unpredictability."

Marcus frowned more so than he already was. "How can you say that at a time like this? I ended up hurting you in my fight with Rubi and I didn't even notice. It took me overhearing your dad complain about it for me to even know." Marcus cringed at the memory and the thought of Zeke's father finding out that he was that armored android. Marcus was sure he suspected it by now. It would be more surprising if he didn't.

"I told ya not to worry about that." Zeke dismissed it with a wave of his hand. "I'm fine. Just a little sore, is all. It's not like we haven't roughed each other up before."

It was true. The two would spar or even get into fights, but never maliciously.

"But it could've been a lot worse. You could be in the hospital or dead. I don't know what the limit of my power is." Marcus sipped on his shake, not wanting to even consider that possibility but his anxious mind left him no choice.

"So? You've always been stronger than me," Zeke pointed out. Getting Marcus to stop worrying was a challenge. Of course, he was more worried about what could happen to others rather than what could happen to him, as usual.

"But I don't know what else is hidden in my code." Maybe he was overthinking this. Maybe he'd seen too many classic robot movies. He was exactly the type of robot that the people in those movies went after.

Zeke sighed, then took a sip from his shake. There didn't seem to be any way to just dismiss this. Zeke didn't like to think of all the bad things that could happen. "I've known ya for five years. I'm sure ya wouldn't do anything to hurt anyone unless they had it coming to 'em. Like those Chimera Elite."

"They trouble me too," Marcus stated. "Do you think they really are who they say they are?" Marcus stared at the sidewalk. While he enjoyed a good mystery, the part he liked was solving it. The lack of clues made this unenjoyable.

"I guess so, 'specially since they had that weird portal tech. We don't have that kind of stuff and no one's heard of the Chimera having it either so it's probably something new that only the higher-ups have access to."

"You're probably right about that. Regular citizens or therians here wouldn't be able to get their hands on experimental tech like that. Only the military would have it. But why are they interested in me? What's so special about me?" Marcus wondered.

"Ya mean besides being the first and only techno-organic android around? Besides the armor?" Zeke listed. "Plus, Dr. Valko was killed by Chimera when the war started, so I'd say they've had their eyes on your family. Still, I couldn't tell ya what their game is or what they're after."

"Me neither. That's what I have to find out. Somehow." Marcus grew quiet, falling deep in thought as he sipped on his shake. He was deemed important enough to have someone sent to spy on him and, not only that, but get close to him. He wondered if it was information they were after. If it was, it didn't make sense that they would have their spy drop the act and attack him before getting any true information and then force someone else to attack the convention he was at. It didn't add up. He couldn't see their goal and that bugged him most of all. "I also have to find Rubi before they do," he added.

"Why do ya even want to help her?" Zeke questioned. "Ya don't know anything about her. She could be trouble."

Marcus took a thoughtful sip. "I know she was being mind-controlled by that lynx-therian somehow. I know she was forced to do what she did. That's all I need to know to help her. And maybe... maybe she has answers." It was worth a shot, anyway. He couldn't think of any other course of action and he didn't want to just do nothing.

"Ya really think so? What if she's just like Azura? What if this is all a trap? She does have the same fire powers and they're both half-therians. They're probably related

107

somehow, maybe part of the same experiment group." Zeke didn't want to see Marcus get hurt again. He was being strong now, but he knew his friend was hurt by learning what Azura really was. He'd probably be focusing more on that if he didn't have these other problems crop up as well.

"I don't know. I won't know unless I find her." He didn't want to think Rubi was the same as Azura. She seemed different somehow, but he wasn't sure he could trust in his own judgment after already being tricked once. Still, he had to try at the very least.

They walked in silence once more, both lost in their own thoughts. This was a troubling situation, no matter what angle one looked at it. Just one of these events would be enough but they came about at the same time. It'd be overwhelming for anyone, but Marcus was managing to hold it together, though his mind raced for answers and his next move.

"Hey, isn't that Rubi?" Zeke asked, breaking the silence, and pointing across the street with his milkshake. Indeed, a deep-skinned girl with dark red hair stood there. She lacked the fox ears and tail, looking fully human, but it was unmistakably her.

Marcus stared for a moment then quickly looked both ways before hurriedly crossing the street. He came up beside her, quietly saying, "Rubi. I've been looking for you. Are you okay?" His expression was that of concern.

He waited for her to acknowledge him, but she thrust her foot square onto the side of his head. Marcus stumbled back, instinctively raising his arms up for the next assault. Her other leg flew at him, but he blocked.

"What are you doing?! Are they controlling you again?!" he demanded, though knew he wouldn't get an answer if she was under mind-control.

Rubi flipped back to get some distance from Marcus. "Who said I needed to be controlled?" she questioned.

"You can talk?!" Why hadn't she before? "What's going on? Are you with the Chimera Elite or not?!"

"You really don't know what's going on, do you? I thought androids were supposed to be intelligent. I guess not." She leaped at him.

Zeke came barreling over and slammed a shoulder into Rubi, knocking her to the ground. "Not today!" he shouted. "I told you she couldn't be trusted."

Rubi started to get up. "If it's not today, it'll be tomorrow. Or the next day. Your time will come eventually."

"Well, if that isn't ominous," Zeke commented.

As Rubi stood up, her body shifted into full therian form. Fur grew all over her body and her ears and tail appeared. Claws were on her fingertips in place of her nails and she had sharp teeth. Marcus took this as a cue to transform into his armor.

"Fine. You want a fight?" Marcus held his fists in front of his chest. "Then you'll have a fight." Marcus rushed at her and threw a punch. She blocked with her arm, a mistake. The fox cartwheeled a few feet away. The arm she used to block hung at her side, in too much pain to function.

Marcus charged again, throwing another punch. This one slammed into a tree as Rubi dodged by flipping backward. Landing on her feet, she glanced at the tree. Bark had exploded off and there was a crater where his fist had landed; cracks ran up and down the tree.

Rubi fled. Fighting Marcus was clearly more trouble than it was worth. She tore down the sidewalk, weaving around gawking pedestrians. Marcus took off after her, the pedestrians moving out of his way in haste.

It soon became too crowded for Rubi to continue running. Food stands lined the road and people were lined up in front of them. A bouquet of smells filled the air, including those from an active hibachi grill.

Marcus tried pushing his way through the crowd, which was surprisingly nonplussed by his armored appearance. Even though he was closer now, it would be harder to get to Rubi. There was also the concern of all the bystanders now present, which would make further fighting more difficult.

Growing fed up with trying to push his way through, Marcus scrambled up a nearby tree. He zeroed in on Rubi's position and vaulted off the tree, coming down on top of her and slamming her to the ground. Marcus grabbed ahold of her while she was stunned. The crowd finally withdrew from the two.

Zeke came out of the crowd, breathing heavily. It had taken him some time to finally catch up with the fleet of foot therian and his android friend. "I see… you finally… caught her," he said between gasps. He was not at all out of shape. They were just that fast.

"Yeah, but now what?" He supposed he should take her to the police, but he just wasn't sure. There was much he wasn't sure of lately.

Rubi forcefully twisted out of Marcus's grasp while he was distracted by Zeke and his own thoughts. She started to take off. Instead of chasing the faster therian again, he charged up a ball of electricity between his hands and launched it straight at her. The electric ball made contact, knocking her off her feet.

She scrambled to her feet, now facing Marcus. Her body twitched from the electricity that still coursed in her. Marcus unleashed a single bolt of electricity. This time, she jumped to avoid it, flipping backward and right into the open fire of the hibachi grill. Pain shot through her body as she realized her mistake and she screamed.

She quickly scrambled off the grill, dropping onto the ground and rolling frantically.

"Wait a minute." Marcus looked toward the singed figure in confusion. "Rubi's not harmed by fire." He marched over to the therian and grabbed her by the neck, holding her up at arm's length. "Who are you?!" he demanded, squeezing tighter. "Why are you disguised as Rubi?!"

The fox therian slowly began changing form, transforming into something else completely. Instead of a fox-therian woman, the person in his grasp now appeared to be a raccoon-dog-therian man.

"Who are you?" Marcus questioned; his voice sounded more surprised now but still with a hint of irritation.

The therian grabbed Marcus's hand and tried to pull it loose from his neck so that he could speak. Marcus grabbed the therian's arm with his free hand and released his neck. "Attempt to escape and I will break your other arm. Remember what happened to the tree."

"Jaron, not that that information will do you any good," he answered, massaging his neck.

"Not giving me information won't do you any good," Marcus threatened. "Just how many of you can shape-shift now?"

"Wouldn't you like to know," Jaron said smugly.

Marcus tightened his grip. "I would," he said, leaning in close to Jaron's face.

"Ah, ah, okay!" Jaron squirmed. "Not many, that I know of. Just me, Azura, and Rubi."

"What do you people want with Marcus, huh?" Zeke demanded. "What's your deal?"

"You sure you want to know?" Jaron wasn't smug this time; he sounded serious.

It made both Marcus and Zeke tense to think what it could be. Marcus spoke up. "Of course, I want to know. Why wouldn't I want to know what's going on?"

"Because it would be too much to handle?" Jaron posed, wicked grin returning to his face. "Do not worry. You'll know soon enough."

A purple pinprick of light appeared and expanded into a large disc. Emerald flame burst from it, followed by a foot that smashed into Marcus' face. He lost his grip on Jaron, who Azura grabbed and hurled into the portal.

"Later, Markie," Azura said as she winked and fell backward into the portal. It promptly disappeared before Marcus could follow after her. He fell on the ground.

"No!" he shouted, pounding his fist on the concrete, cracking it. They just kept getting away without any leads. How was he supposed to figure anything out if the keepers of some of his answers were continually beyond his grasp?

Zeke outstretched a hand. "We should get going before the crowd stops staring and starts asking questions."

Marcus accepted the assistance and stood up. "Good idea. I narrowly avoided that at the convention." Marcus looked over the crowd to find the best exit. "Wish we had one of those portals." He narrowed his vision to an alleyway with a fire escape. "Let's split up. I'll get out of here faster by myself and you don't have armor so you can disappear easier."

"Got it." Zeke nodded and gave a smile. "I'll message you when I find a safe spot."

Marcus nodded in return, then turned and dashed for the alleyway. He climbed up the fire escape and ran across the roof. He'd probably have to hop a few roofs to keep everyone from following him.

Landing on a rooftop, Marcus realized he was not alone. A figure with leathery wings landed on the same roof. It was Nox, a bat therian and one of Marcus's friends. He folded his wings behind him.

"Is that really you Marcus?" he questioned as he stroked one of his ears. "I saw you with Zeke. It sounds like you."

Marcus was silent. After a few moments, he spoke up. "It's me."

"Why did you tell Zeke?" Nox's voice was always soft and never seemed to be angry; not even now. "And not me?" He seemed more like a child who had done something wrong than someone who was upset at his friend keeping a secret.

"I didn't want to get my friends caught up this, whatever it is." Marcus gazed at his palm as if it would hold answers; it, of course, didn't. "Zeke's just persistent. You know that." Marcus went on to detail each time he transformed and the

"This is a predicament," Nox observed, stroking his ear again.

"That's an understatement." Marcus wasn't even sure how big of a deal this was. He doubted it was simply nothing but wasn't sure how life-changing it could be. "And you're not freaked out by any of this?"

"Well, maybe a little. It's hard for me to be freaked out by much." Nox looked off into the distance as if he were remembering some event. "We were taught to fear and hate battle androids—or any androids—in the Regime, but I know you're my friend."

"That's true but…" Marcus turned and took a step forward to leave. "This armor is the result of coding hidden in my systems. What other programming is hiding there?"

Nox watched silently as his friend leaped to another rooftop and then another, not having an answer. Marcus disappeared down a fire escape as he transformed into his regular form. Nox's ears drooped. Marcus had helped him so much in the past. He wished he could help his friend with this, but he didn't see how he could.

"You could've been a little nicer," Jaron griped from his place on the floor. "That stupid robot broke my arm!"

Azura spun around and kicked Jaron square in the face. He slid across the floor.

"My nose!" he cried. "What was that for?"

"You were going to spill everything!" she accused, stalking toward him.

"What? No! I was not!" He frantically waved a hand in front of him. "I was just... talking! Buying time! He could've killed me!"

Azura grabbed him by the neck and slammed him into the wall, holding him there. "So could I."

"Azura!" came a shout. Randor entered the room. "Put him down!"

"But, Randor, he-"

"Now!" he boomed, using a fraction of his sonic scream to amplify his voice.

Azura quickly put Jaron down and stepped back.

"My father may believe in killing soldiers for their failures, but it does not improve morale. We'd soon have no soldiers left." Randor paced over to Azura, stopping just in front of her face. "We learn from mistakes, but they can't learn if they're killed after just one. Do I make myself clear?"

"Yes, sir," Azura mumbled.

"Good." Randor backed away. It wasn't an entirely satisfactory response, but he knew it was all he would get out of her. "Besides, shapeshifters are at a premium. He's too valuable to just terminate." Randor touched two fingers at the base of his ear, activating his comm. "Neva. Get up here and tend to Jaron's wounds."

It wasn't long before Neva entered the room with a medkit. She knelt by Jaron and began patching him up, starting by applying a spray-on cast to his arm.

"Let's leave her to her work," Randor ordered, stepping out of the room, Azura following behind him. "We need to be prepared for our next move."

CHAPTER 7

"So, how're we gonna explain this to Marcus?" Zeke asked. He was sitting in his desk chair. His room was disorganized, laundry scattered throughout and several things not in their place.

"What do you mean we?" Nox questioned, sitting in a bean bag chair on

125

the floor. His arms were crossed, his knees were pulled in, and his wings were folded at his sides. "It was your idea to keep this a secret in the first place. Why not just tell him?"

Rubi sat in another bean bag chair, munching on chicken nuggets like they were some rare delicacy. Zeke had Nox pick them up when he called him over. If Nox had known that this is what Zeke wanted them for, he might've just brought Marcus with him, but he had long since stopped asking Zeke why. It was usually better that he did not know.

"Because he's got too much going on! The armor, the Chimera Elite, Azura... He probably can't think straight right now. I gotta make sure Rubi here isn't another Azura. I mean, how do we even know she actually exists?" Zeke explained.

"Um, she's sitting right there," Nox pointed out, not understanding what his friend meant.

"Oh, I know someone's sitting there but with all the shapeshifters lately, how can you tell it's actually her? That could be Azura there or that raccoon guy. We don't know. We also don't know if Rubi is an actual person or just someone they made up. Ya follow?" Zeke asked.

Nox looked over at Rubi, pondering what Zeke had said. "I guess so. She could just be a persona they created to manipulate Marcus. We have no way to verify it."

Rubi's ear twitched. Even though she seemed oblivious while snacking on the nuggets, she had heard everything and had understood everything. She realized that it was difficult for them to trust her even though Marcus had shared that she had been mind-controlled at the convention. In response to their query, she held up a hand brought forth vermilion flames.

The two watched, wondering for a moment if she was going to attack. The flames soon died out as she extinguished them and returned to her meal. She then resumed seemingly ignoring them.

"What do ya think that means?" Zeke questioned his friend.

"Didn't Marcus mention that Azura had green flames? Maybe she's using it as an identifier? The fire at the convention was orange," Nox suggested.

"Yeah, and that raccoon wasn't immune to fire like Rubi or Azura is, so he's probably not a pyro. I guess it is her and she's a separate person. Well, that's figured out now, but we still don't know what side she's on and she's not exactly talkative," Zeke griped.

"Maybe she's not sure about us either. She's been used once that we know of," Nox suggested. He had his own trust issues.

"Guess you're right about that, still... Just 'cause she's not on their side doesn't mean that she's on our side," Zeke said. He wasn't normally this suspicious about people, but the stakes were higher than usual. It was quite possibly life or death.

They were both quiet. Nox studied Rubi, wondering what might have happened to her in the past. Had she escaped the Chimera Regime as he and his mother did? Where were her parents? Did they get killed during the escape like his father? Was she someone important enough that the Chimera prince and his team were sent to bring her back? Was she one of their experiments perhaps? Was that the explanation for her pyrokinesis and shapeshifting? It was the only explanation he could conceive of.

"So…" Zeke broke the silence. "How're we gonna tell Marcus?"

Nox laid his head back on the bean bag chair and let out an exasperated sigh.

"Any leads yet?"

"No, Marcus, there aren't any leads. Besides, I'm on required leave right now," Nova answered. Androids were also given leave after major injuries or, like Nova, technically dying. It didn't affect them as much as it would a human, but it was still safer to give them time to adjust to it as even androids could become unstable.

"I know." Marcus was sprawled out on the couch, looking horribly bored. "I'm just tired of waiting around for them to attack me again. I'd like to have the upper hand for once and to figure out what they're after."

Nova did not respond, simply changing through the channels on the television, which took up most of the wall parallel to the couch. He could not offer any suggestions or advice on the matter. Sharing anything with Marcus could prove dangerous and it wasn't like he had been listening to his advice so far.

Marcus got off the couch and took a step toward the door. He wasn't getting anywhere here.

"Where are you going?" Nova asked, finally settling on a news station.

"Out," Marcus replied before exiting the room.

Nova watched from the couch, contemplating in silence, wondering if he should go after him. It wouldn't do any good. Nothing's ever been able to stop him once he's set out to do something; especially back then. Nova felt uneasy about all of this. He hated keeping secrets from his brother, but he knew what the consequences could be if he shared anything. Not just for Marcus, but for everyone.

Marcus sat on a bistro outside of an ice cream parlor, casually eating a bowl of brownie batter ice cream. He had his almost shoulder-length hair down instead of in its usual ponytail. He was also wearing a baseball hat and a pair of sunglasses. It was a horrible disguise, and he knew it but maybe, if the Chimera Elite were roaming around here, they wouldn't notice him right away.

Despite being the brother of a police officer, he didn't know much about how to find leads as he had never really taken much of an interest and, although having a strong sense of justice and willingness to help people, law enforcement never really appealed to him as a career. He felt he wanted something more but could never quite figure out what that was. He was starting to wonder if it was more than just fantasizing about adventure but something from his past calling to him instead.

"Hey, Marcus!" someone greeted, whom Marcus realized was Zeke by his voice. "Figured you'd be here. Ya always come here to think or relax."

"Hey, Zeke, Nox," Marcus said with less enthusiasm, having looked up to see the two. "What were you looking for me for?"

"Just wondering how you're holding up," Zeke replied, taking a seat.

Nox laid his ears back. "Enough with the small talk, Zeke. Just tell him."

"Tell me what?" Marcus inquired, putting a spoonful of ice cream in his mouth. What did Zeke do now?

"Zeke found Rubi," Nox answered for him. "He's been hiding her in his room."

Marcus blinked. At first, he wasn't sure how to process this information or how to react to it. He had been searching for her whenever he had the chance, even looking for anyone mentioning an unusual fox-therian online. He supposed he should be angry with Zeke, but he was just so relieved that Rubi was found that he completely skipped over that emotion.

Rubi, in her half-therian form, stepped into view. She was wearing a lilac baseball cap, a purple pullover jacket, and white capris tucked into the same purple boots she had been in before. Besides her shoes, Marcus recognized the rest of the clothes as belonging to his sister; it seemed she was in on this too. As Rubi was much shorter than his sister, the jacket was quite baggy, looking more like a dress on her.

She sat down close to Marcus, facing the street, eyes darting all over the surrounding area like someone would jump out to capture her at any second. Nox sat down across from her so that most of her would be obscured by his body, though he was about the same height as her and didn't offer that much coverage outside of his tall ears and wings. They all leaned in to talk quietly.

"Why did you run away?" Marcus asked in a whisper. "They learned that you were being mind-controlled when you attacked the convention."

Marcus got out his phone and placed it in front of Rubi so that she could use it to communicate with as before. She looked down at the phone and then away.

"Cannot leave Chimera Elite," she spoke painstakingly as if every word took a Herculean effort. Her voice was but a whisper.

"Why not?" Zeke asked just a bit too loud, getting looks from both Marcus and Zeke.

Rubi was silent for a few moments. Everyone waited quietly for her to speak again. Finally, she did. "They have a friend."

"They're holding a friend of yours hostage to keep you cooperating when the mind-control doesn't work?" Marcus echoed to make sure he understood.

Rubi nodded. "Already gone too long. May already be too late."

Marcus put a hand to his chin in thought for a moment, going over everything he'd learned so far, from this conversation and before. "It's settled then," he spoke. "We're going to rescue your friend."

"We're what? Hold on!" Zeke contested.

"They are the Chimera Elite, led by the heir himself," Nox reminded Marcus. "They are likely extremely well-trained fighters, as you've already found out for yourself. Also, we have no idea where they're hiding out. Since they have the capability to create portals, they could likely be anywhere, even Mars."

"I know this," Marcus said. "And I don't care. This armor and my electrical abilities were obviously meant for taking on

Chimera. You two don't have to come. It can be just me and Rubi."

"Yeah, you have the armor and powers, but you've never used them before! You don't have training like they do! And the two of you'll be outnumbered! It's insane!" Zeke argued.

"You're always talking me into doing crazy stuff. What's changed?" Marcus questioned.

"The high chance of dying!" Zeke answered.

Marcus didn't have a comeback. He knew the risks fully, but he was tired of waiting around while the Chimera Elite came after him, while they hurt people. He was itching to take the fight to them.

"It'll probably be safer for you at my house," Marcus spoke to Rubi. "There're more people able to protect you and it wouldn't be good for Zeke's dad to find you. He's... overzealous."

"Meaning he'd probably try to turn you over to the police," Zeke added.

Rubi grew nervous at the prospect of being apprehended.

"Don't worry. I checked with Nova, my brother who's a police officer. He said charges against you were dropped," Marcus assured. "But they want you for questioning, which I'm guessing you're not up for."

Rubi shook her head. She didn't want to be held here. She had to rescue her friend and get back home. "Lynx-therian is Neva," she shared, thinking it might be useful to know. "Only survivor of an experiment to make telepaths. Dangerous but has limits. Can only control organics, not machines."

"Well, that's good news. For me anyway. You're still vulnerable." Marcus needed Rubi in order to find her friend but wasn't sure about risking her being mind-controlled again.

"I can fight it. Didn't before because they would hurt my friend." Rubi seemed more comfortable speaking to them; perhaps she trusted their intentions now.

"Alright. Then you and I will go as soon as you're up to it," Marcus stated. He was itching to ruin the Chimera Elite's day and plans just as they had been ruining his.

"We'll go too!" Zeke announced.

"We?" Nox questioned, side-eying Zeke.

"Neva could take over either of you two," Marcus pointed out. "It wouldn't be a good idea."

"Nonsense! While you two are busy going toe-to-toe with the Chimera, we can sneak around to get Rubi's mate." Zeke looked immensely proud of his idea. "It's not like ya can do both at the same time."

"I guess that's a solid plan," Marcus conceded, "and I know there's no talking you out of it."

"I suppose I could help navigate," Nox offered reluctantly. This was more than what he usually got talked into doing, but he didn't want his friends to go off alone. Rather, he didn't want them to leave him behind.

"Thank you," Rubi said as she bowed her head.

"No problem," Marcus said as held up a fist. "I've been waiting to stick it to those guys."

CHAPTER 8

The group had gone to Marcus's place as
being out in the open made Rubi uneasy.
The Chimera Elite had a higher chance of
finding her and there was also the
possibility of someone recognizing her from
the convention. Being in her half-therian
form rather than her full therian form didn't

guarantee her going unnoticed. Her ears and tail were the same as was her build. Plus, any other therians present would be able to identify her by scent.

They rested, waiting until dark to get ready for the rescue mission. They couldn't let anyone know what they were about to do, lest they try to stop them. They had to be the ones to rescue Rubi's friend. There'd be too many questions if they went to the police and they'd probably take too long.

"Is everybody ready?" Marcus whispered. He wasn't in his armor yet as that would draw too much attention.

They all nodded.

"Then let's go."

The four came to a vacant building. It was a solid building, but it needed some work; it didn't look like anyone had been there in a long time. A fitting place for a hideout. No one would pay any attention to such an old building.

"So, how're we getting inside?" Zeke whispered.

"We break in." Marcus pounded his fist into the open palm of his other hand.

"That is a really bad plan," Nox pointed out, ears drooping in exasperation. "They'll know we're here."

"They'll know I'm here," Marcus corrected. "They'll know Rubi and I am here. As soon as we're in and they're focused on us, you two sneak in and look for Rubi's friend. Just like we planned."

"She's in the basement. Entrance is right inside the door. Chimera Elite are upstairs." Rubi was flexing her fingers, apparently preparing to use her flames. That's what they all assumed anyway since that's where they always seem to come from.

"Alright. So, are we all ready?" Marcus looked to each of them, who each gave a nod. "Okay. Here we go." He smashed his fist right into the boarded-up door. It cracked and splintered, crumbling to nothing. Marcus and Rubi jumped inside first, blasting a barrage of electricity and flame to cover for Zeke and Nox, who slipped by behind them and to the basement door.

"Randor!" Marcus shouted, stomping in the direction Rubi indicated they would be. He made every effort to be as loud as possible. There was no way anyone there could've not noticed. He went up the dark staircase, Rubi following behind him. After rounding a corner, he could see a faint light.

He cut down the electricity, restricting it just to sparks on his hands. He'd need it for the battle, and he wasn't sure of his limits just yet. He assumed the electricity he generated came from his core and it was not good for that to run out of power completely. It could result in programming damage.

Rubi had restricted her flames to her hands before Marcus had cut down on his powers. There was no need to burn the building down before she could get her friend out. Though afterward, perhaps they should burn it down so that the police would investigate. The Chimera Elite wouldn't stop just because they lost a building.

They could hear movement beyond the stairs. It was clear that more than one person was up there. Shortly, only one set of footsteps were heard coming toward the door to the stairs. Marcus and Rubi readied themselves. Randor stepped out but did not make the move to attack.

"Why are you here?" Randor asked as if this was a mere annoyance. He did not seem alarmed.

"For answers!" Marcus's fists grew tight. "And for what you did to my brother!"

"Answers, hmm?" Randor grinned, showing off his sharp teeth. "What makes you think I'd give you any? Or that you could even handle them?"

"It doesn't matter! I'm tired of being in the dark!" Marcus started running toward him. "I'll just beat it out of you!" He leaped at Randor; a sparking fist ready to pound into the wolf-therian's face. Randor didn't flinch as the android approached, he just inhaled then unleashed a sonic blast from his jaws.

Marcus and Rubi both tumbled down the stairs, hitting the wall where the stairs took a turn. Marcus forced himself up and threw himself at Randor again, who released another sonic blast, smashing Marcus into the wall again. Rubi stayed down against the wall, hands covering her ears. Fighting Randor had always been a difficult task. His sonic booms could blow out her flames in a second. How many times would Marcus charge at him?

Finally, he stayed down on his hands and knees. How could he defeat an opponent when he couldn't even stay on his feet? How did Randor even have such power? More experiments like with Azura, Rubi, and Jaron? It seemed like the Chimera were making themselves stronger and that could only mean one thing. They were planning to attack earth again.

"As much fun as this is, you're clearly not ready yet, Dynamo. But don't worry. We'll have a proper fight when you remember." A portal opened behind Randor and he let himself fall backwards into it.

Marcus charged forward but the portal disappeared before he could get there, causing him to fall on the steps. His frustration, which was already high, was mounting. He felt powerless in this situation. What was he to do? The answers he wanted kept slipping from his grasp.

Rubi stood up and started down the steps. She had to check on her friend and how her rescuers were doing. The others disappearing did not bode well. Marcus' friends did not have special powers to defend themselves with.

Marcus, getting the hint, followed her. He was starting to think this whole thing was a bad idea. Why didn't he just tell the police where they were so they could take care of it? Then he'd have to explain how he learned of their location. Him knowing Rubi before the attack could lead to unfortunate implications as well as him having contact with her after and not informing the police when they wanted her for questioning. She wasn't a normal therian, and he was sure someone would want to perform tests on her. Or, perhaps, he simply watched too many movies.

They arrived in the basement to find Nox and Zeke on the ground. Another bat-therian, darkly colored, stood across from them, her wings out and fanning back and forth. Her long tail caught Marcus's eye as unusual, then he noticed a pair of short horns on her head. Were all the Chimera Elite the result of experiments?

"Are you guys okay?" Marcus asked, looking down at his friends.

"I think so." Zeke rubbed his head. "I don't know how, but she just knocked us down. Didn't even get close to us."

Nox got onto his knees. "It was like we were just pulled to the floor."

"My fire won't reach her," Rubi spoke. "Too dangerous to use down here."

"I bet this'll reach her!" Marcus let loose a blast of electricity. It hit its mark and she began falling backward. A portal opened under her and she disappeared through it. It quickly closed. "Blast! Now they've all escaped!"

Rubi wasted no time hurrying over to the cage her friend was kept in. A badger-therian with lilac gray fur was inside, curled up and lying on her side. Rubi grabbed the bars and melted them. She pulled her friend out of the cage. She was breathing shallowly and felt both cold and light. Rubi, carrying her friend, walked back over to the others.

"Well, we got what we came for anyway," Marcus said, though he had hoped to get more. "Let's go before something else happens."

"Wait," Nox spoke up. "We should check for any information or clues they might've left."

"Good idea. We might find some answers after all." Marcus felt somewhat better that this wouldn't be a total loss for him.

They made their way back up the stairs to the ground floor, then started up the staircase to the second floor. Rubi stopped. "Wait."

The others followed suit. The reason became clear as green flames spilled down the staircase. Everyone turned and ran down the stairs as fast as they could, diving out the hole Marcus had made earlier. Once outside, they quickly ducked into an alleyway.

Rubi handed her friend off to Zeke and stood at the entrance of the alleyway. Her hands were held out toward the building and she seemed deeply focused. The fire wasn't dying but it appeared to be contained to the building. Sirens were heard in the distance.

"Come on, Rubi!" Marcus insisted. "They'll take care of it. If they find you here, even if the flames aren't the right color, they'll assume you did it!"

Rubi stayed where she was. The sirens grew closer.

"We have to go!" Marcus wrapped an arm around Rubi's midsection and ran into the alleyway, the others having already started to flee. Rubi released control of the flames and became limp. She was still conscious, just spent.

With everyone's attention on the building engulfed in emerald flames, it was easy for them to slip away unnoticed. They soon arrived at the Valko mansion. It wasn't uncommon for Zeke and Nox to stay over, so that was their cover.

"You're back awful late. In your armor. And with an injured therian." Nova turned on the entry room light. "And the fox-therian who attacked the convention. Also, I hear of a building on fire with green flames."

So much for being discreet. Marcus should have known that Nova wouldn't be oblivious.

"I can explain," Marcus started.

"I should hope so." Nova walked over to the group, looking over the badger-therian whom Zeke was still holding. He wasn't a doctor, but he had more medical knowledge than the average person from his police training. "She's very ill, likely malnourished."

"The Chimera Elite had her. She's a friend of Rubi's." Marcus was still holding Rubi as well. She seemed exhausted.

"I may be on leave, but I still have duties," Nova lectured. "You should have come to me about this."

Marcus' gaze sank to the floor. He knew it was risky, but everyone had agreed to take the risk. He didn't want to wait. What if Rubi's friend had died in the meantime?

"Oh, don't be so harsh, brother," a feminine voice came from the other room.

Nebula stepped into view. "He just did what you would've done. Don't you have a tendency to disregard orders to save people?"

Nova was silent. He had no rebuttal for that for it was true. He had, on more than one occasion, abandoned protocol to rescue people. Some disliked it; an android disobeying his orders so easily. Others loved it as it proved androids were not heartless machines that would just follow orders even when they were wrong.

"The poor things," Nebula cooed once she got a good look at the two therians. "We should be taking care of them instead of arguing."

Nova relented, leaving to fetch the first aid kit. Nebula beckoned for the two to follow as she went to the living room. "Just lay them down on the couch." The double-Lshaped couch took up the entire wall opposite the television. Marcus gently laid Rubi down on the end of the couch, Zeke putting the other therian down nearby.

Nebula went to tend to Rubi first, but as she got close, the fox-therian coughed and said in a strained voice, "Marin. Marin first."

She tended to the badger-therian instead, taking her temperature and checking other vital signs. "She's definitely caught something. Hasn't had enough to drink or eat either. She'll need lots of rest."

Nova entered the room, handing his sister the kit. "I'll need some cold medicine too," she said. Nova left the room again.

Rubi sat up and started to fall over, Marcus catching her before she did. "Whoa, you need to just stay still," he warned.

"Marin," Rubi whispered, reaching out her hand in her direction. "Marin…"

"Don't worry. She'll be okay so long as she gets some rest and nutrition," Nebula said as she helped Marin drink some medicine, then adding, "which you also need. So just lie back down."

Rubi didn't lie down, but she did let her body relax in Marcus' arms. She was completely exhausted, but she couldn't just rest. Her friend needed to be taken care of and although someone else was already doing that, she felt she had to do something. This wouldn't have happened if not for her.

"I'll go make some soup," Zeke volunteered, leaving for the kitchen. Nox followed to help him.

"I'll be right back," Nebula announced, leaving the room momentarily. She returned with two blankets, giving one to Rubi. The other, which was an electric blanket, she draped over Marin and plugged it in. "Her temperature needs to be kept up or she'll get worse."

Marcus finally decided to switch out of his armor, having nearly forgotten he was even in it. He grabbed some TV trays and set them up beside Rubi and Marin so that there'd be a place to set the soup when it was ready. He returned to sit by Rubi.

Although they had rescued her friend, Marcus felt like he hadn't done enough. The Chimera Elite had all gotten away, and he still didn't have any answers. He didn't know what tomorrow would bring, but he was sure this was far from over.

CHAPTER 9

It was the next morning. What time it was, Rubi wasn't sure. It could be afternoon for all she knew. She felt like she had slept for quite some time. The half-therian just lied there for a while. Being able to rest in a relatively safe and comfortable environment was a rarity. She couldn't remember the last time she had. After some time of silence, she sat up and looked over at Marin. The young badger-therian was sleeping and seemed to be in a state of peace despite her sickness.

Marcus entered the room, carrying a plate of food. He set it down on the TV near Rubi. "I'm no gourmet cook, but it's edible. I hope."

She looked at the plate and gave it a sniff. On it was scrambled eggs, bacon, and toast with jam. A fairly standard breakfast, not that Rubi knew anything of standard. Back on Mars, in the Resistance, one ate whatever one could find. Breakfast was jerky and dried fruit. So was lunch and dinner if you were lucky.

The half-therian picked up the fork and began eating, chewing the food thoroughly and savoring it. "Thank you," she whispered in-between bites.

"Don't worry about it." Marcus stood there, awkwardly watching her. A lot had happened, and he had found few answers. She may not be able to tell him about his armor, but she could tell him more about the Chimera Elite. "So... what do you know about the Chimera Elite?"

Rubi's chewing became slow at the question. She waited until she swallowed to speak. "They are a team of powerful Chimera picked by Randor for special missions that require special talents."

"Like telepaths and shape-shifters?"

"Yes." Rubi took another bite, then continued. "Jaron's shape-shifting surpasses my own. He can appear as anyone. Azura isn't as advanced as him, but more advanced than me. We're limited to a few forms and variations of our original appearance, but she isn't stuck with her tails and ears like me."

"I was wondering about that since you both shape-shift and have fire powers. Were you part of the same batch? Like how they experimented on Neva?" he questioned.

Rubi didn't answer. Marcus stood there uncomfortably in the silence. So much for earning her trust. "What about that... bat-like creature? Another experiment?"

"Yes," she answered this time. "Kyrie."

Marcus nodded. Not a lot of information but he'd take what he could get for now. Perhaps Rubi would spill more later if she felt comfortable, so he wasn't going to press and make her feel cornered. The last thing he wanted to do right now was take his frustrations out on someone else who was having her own problems. Plus, she may not share if she didn't feel it was safe to. He had to convince her that he wasn't her enemy.

He turned on the TV for a distraction, purposefully avoiding any news stations and deciding cartoons were safe to leave on. The android sat quietly, not actually paying them any attention. He just kept going over the recent events and what he had found out so far, trying to find something he may have missed. There was a connection between his armored form and the appearance of the Chimera Elite, of that he was sure, but he didn't know what the connection may be.

It must've been an hour or more that Marcus just sat there as Rubi had long finished her breakfast and wandered off to find the restroom. Also, there was a different cartoon on. He was about to get up and see if she got lost when the half-therian came flying into the room and landed hard on the ground.

"What?" Marcus stood up quickly to look through the doorway. He saw a strange android, one in armor not unlike his own but teal and white in color with orange lights. He also had an orange visor attached to his helmet. There were large glowing circles on his wrists that Marcus assumed to be part of a weapon system.

Marcus wasted no time in switching to his own armor, standing firmly in front of Rubi and clenching his fists, electricity dancing around them. The attacker stopped his approach and relaxed his stance for a moment, seeming surprised though it was hard for Marcus to tell since half of his face was covered by his visor. "You should know better, Dynamo. That therian is the enemy! She even killed Nova!"

"Oh, yeah?" He skipped asking how the android knew that name. "Rubi here was being mind-controlled and Nova's better now."

"Mind-controlled?" he scoffed. "You expect me to believe that?"

"Maybe," Marcus shrugged. "How about you start telling me who you are and how you got past security?"

"That should be obvious." The intruder pointed to his chest where an orange "V" shape that resembled Marcus' own was; the Valroid symbol. "I'm Magneto if you really don't remember; your younger brother and fellow member of the now-disbanded Team Eclipse, a special group of battle androids formed to defeat the Chimera Regime twenty years ago."

"Team Eclipse? What are you talking about? That can't be right. I'm not twenty. I was only brought online five years ago." Though even as he said it, Marcus doubted the truth of that statement now. It was hard to know what the truth was anymore.

"So, she erased your memory? I suppose I shouldn't be surprised. Masumi never cared about us. We were only tools to avenge her dead husband." Magneto flipped his visor up, revealing a burnt face and damaged eyes. "I lost my eyes for a human I never met! I was made only by her, only to fight Chimera. Now I have to use this visor to see and it's not as good as android eyes."

Marcus blinked, taking in this new information. He knew that Dr. Valko had been killed when the war between earth and the Chimera Regime began, but he had never heard of "Team Eclipse". That was entirely new to him.

"Why didn't you just get your eyes fixed or replaced?" Marcus questioned, folding his arms. It didn't seem like Magneto intended to attack him. "It's not like Mom's short on money."

"Haven't you been listening? She doesn't care and I don't trust her. Just look at you." Magneto gestured to Marcus. "You don't remember me or Eclipse. She erased your memory and you still want to call her "mom"?"

"I don't know that. You don't know that." Marcus had to admit, though, that it was becoming hard to trust her. It was clear that something was being kept secret and she wouldn't tell him.

"You don't not know that," Magneto countered. "Fine. If you want to trust her, that's your problem and if you want to make friends with the enemy, that's fine too."

Rubi walked around Marcus and stood to face Magneto. "I am not your enemy," she said in a quiet but firm tone. "I fight your enemy, the Chimera. I'm a member of the Resistance on Mars."

Magneto huffed and waved his hand in dismissal, no longer wanting to argue about any of this. He left the room and then the house. Marcus didn't move, not seeing a point in chasing him down. Could this get any weirder? What was the point in him coming if he was just going to be defeated so easily?

"The Resistance?" he finally spoke. "You hadn't mentioned that before."

"Hadn't felt it necessary." Rubi pulled the turtleneck of her shirt over her mouth. "I cannot stay here. I must return. I'm... the only super-powered one in the Resistance. I'm afraid... they don't stand a chance without me."

Marcus was silent. Fire powers and shapeshifting aside, he never would've imagined this small therian was part of a resistance. He thought she was just an escaped Chimera experiment. She probably still was one as he could think of no other reason that she'd have those powers, but she probably escaped a long time ago and then joined the resistance.

"Why don't you come with us?" a weak voice from the couch asked. Marin had stirred, hearing the whole conversation. "Since you've fought the Chimera before, you could help us."

"M-mars?" Marcus had been caught off guard, not expecting that the badger-therian was awake. "I can't go to Mars. I have no way to get there. We don't have commercial flights to Mars. I... can't help you." He also had too much going on himself. He had to figure out what he was going to do about these recent revelations of his past. What else was mother hiding? How long could he keep this secret from the rest of the world?

Rubi lowered her head, eyes closed. She was afraid there was no way to get back to Mars. No one ever wanted to get back to Mars. Everyone wanted to escape from Mars, to leave that awful place behind and never look back. But she couldn't, there were people counting on her.

Masumi slumped down in her chair, exhausted from her normal work plus the extra damage control she had to do concerning "Dynamo" and the events of the expo. Reaching under her desk, she pulled out a bottle of sake and a shot glass she had hidden. She poured some into the small glass and took a sip.

"Drinking at work now, Masumi?"

She inhaled and choked on her drink, spilling some from the glass. She looked over to a dark corner of her office to see Dr. Gates. He was holding a piece of red metal.

"What are you doing here?!" she accused, setting down her shot glass. "How did you get past security?"

"Old friends, remember? You know, I was always curious about your little techno-organic marvel. An android that could not only eat but needed nutrition. An android that didn't just reboot its systems but needed sleep. An android that not only had a bionic lung to cool its systems but needed to breathe."

"What are you getting at?" The recent events and her tiredness were making her defensive and more agitated than usual.

"I always wondered how you did it. You're a programmer, a darn good one, but you're not a biologist or a doctor. You're not even a bioengineer. And you're not the kind to outsource when it comes to building your own androids, not even to others within your own company."

Masumi frowned, more than she already was, and poured more sake into her glass.

"But now that I know Marcus is actually Dynamo, I know exactly how you did it," Gates stated as he held up the piece of metal, the one that had broken off of Marcus' helmet at the expo, "because I helped you do it."

Gates tossed the piece onto her desk. Masumi looked at it, then emptied her shot glass in one gulp. She leaned under her desk and pulled out another shot glass, now filling both and sliding one toward Gates. After a moment of hesitation, he picked it up.

Masumi spun her chair to the side, leaning an elbow on her desk. "Yes, Marcus is that poor boy who came to us barely alive, who Audric contacted you to save."

Gates chuckled. "You two were always so ambitious, it's not surprising. After all, it was you and Audric who created a fully functioning android as your senior project, and a revolutionary one at that." He was speaking of Nova, the first of the Valroids.

"I guess you are right at that." A tired smile crept across Masumi's face as she reminisced old times. Simpler times when she and Audric were just engaged, still in college, and with their whole lives ahead of them. Her smile faded as she recalled how Audric's was cut short.

"We could both get into a lot of trouble if any of this gets out." Gates broke the silence and took a sip.

"I know. Why do you think I'm so tired? I've been working the past several days trying to fix this. The reporters are relentless. I've had to double security." It was a complete disaster. Dynamo was an unaccounted for, unregistered android. Marcus was registered, but it would cause more problems to say they were one and the same. Why would Valko Industries make a battle android, they would ask.

"This is too big to just sweep under the rug, especially with the Chimera's involvement. You know they're here for a reason. You may want to make plans for when this does get out." Gates sat down the empty glass and walked out the door.

Masumi sat her glass down, tears rolling down her face.

CHAPTER 10

Marcus had gone to his favorite coffee shop to think. It was not an easy place to be considering how many dates he and Azura had been on there. They had gotten to meeting there so regularly, like clockwork. This was certainly not one of Marcus' normal times to be there, but he did not feel like going to any of his other haunts. The ice cream shop would be busier this time of day, and he didn't feel like playing VR games or browsing the astronomy section of the library. He'd read all those books already anyway. No, he needed to simply sit and think, only sipping a cup of cappuccino and bouncing his leg on the floor.

His deep focus was broken only by hearing someone speak the word "dynamo". It came from the television mounted on the wall of the café. It was the reporter on the local news.

"...have been looking into the case of this mysterious armored android. The Valroid "V" symbol is clear on his chest, connecting him to Valko Industries, the producer of the Valroid model of androids. Our investigations, including a tip from an anonymous source, have revealed that this Dynamo is actually Marcus Valko, android son of Masumi Valko, the CEO of Valko Industries, and her late husband Dr. Audric Valko." A photo of Marcus was shown on screen.

Several eyes shifted to his position.

"As for why the Valkos built a battle android in secret or why this form was only revealed now, we do not know. We will continue with our investigation and we will look into any relation to the attack at the Tech Convention and the attack at the hospital that resulted in the escape of the two therian suspects."

Marcus did not have to look to know that all eyes were on him; he could feel them burning into his being. He could hear them begin to whisper about the news report, about the battle armor, about the Chimera.

There would be no peaceful thinking here. Marcus gulped down the rest of his cappuccino. He took a deep breath, exhaling audibly through his nostrils and stood up to leave. He crushed his empty cup and threw it in the trash as he walked out.

He walked somberly down the sidewalk, no destination in mind. The worst had just happened, it seemed, but he felt nothing. Nothing but a quiet annoyance and frustration. So much had already happened, but now his newfound secret was out to the world. There would be no hiding, no figuring out what to do about this in private. Would they come for him like in all the old monster stories? He was dangerous, an unknown factor.

Mars was starting to sound like a better idea. He could escape all the questions, all the paparazzi, and do what he was clearly built to do: fight. Looking back, he did always enjoy a fight scene, an epic battle, but who didn't? He did always enjoy a good battle in the VR, but who didn't? He also had had a tendency to get into fights at school, never over trivialities, but to protect his classmates from bullies. It had always seemed especially important to him to fight for those who couldn't. That's how he met Nox, a poor orphaned therian who had managed to escape the horrors of the Martian prisons, though his father had died in the initial escape attempt and his mother had died of failing health after reaching earth. The bat-therian had had no one to look after him and was too broken from the horrors he had faced to have the strength to fight back. Marcus had had no problem finding the strength to fight for him, rather liking his role of protector of his bullied classmates. Perhaps he had enjoyed getting into fights after all but would only do so if given a proper reason. Though he and Zeke would sometimes spar for fun; his friend was surprisingly strong for a human.

Marcus' thought-fueled wandering took him by a small electronics repair store. There were previously broken televisions in the window to show off the shopkeeper's handiwork. The news was on, but the focus was not on him anymore, it had shifted to his mother. There was an image of her shown by the newscaster with the word "KIDNAPPED" plastered over it. At first, it didn't register.

"...but we do not yet know why Valko Industries CEO Masumi Valko was kidnapped by the same two therians who snuck into Mecha City University Hospital.

The suspects are a brown, male wolf-therian and a blue, female fox-therian with three tails. They have access to an unknown technology that creates a "portal", which looks like a purple disc floating in the air. This is the footage of the kidnapping."

The screen switched to a security camera feed from inside Valko Industries. The portal opened, Randor and Azura stepping out. Masumi initially tried to fend them off by grabbing her cane, which hid a sword inside; Marcus had gotten his interest in kendo and swords from her. She didn't stand a chance against the two, however, as Randor used his sonic scream to knock her into the wall. Azura carried her unconscious form through the portal. Before leaving himself, Randor turned to face the security camera. As he backed into the portal, the wolf therian said, "See you on Mars, hero."

The broadcast returned to the newscaster, who mused about the implication of Masumi being taken to Mars and wondering who the hero was that Randor was speaking to. Marcus already knew who it was. That had been a direct message to him.

"Well, I guess I'm going to Mars."

When Marcus got home, the living room lights were off, but he found Nova sitting on the couch. Sensing that Nova had been waiting for him by his serious aura, Marcus stepped into the room but didn't turn on the light. Instead of greeting his brother, he simply waited for Nova's words.

"I got you a shuttle to Mars," Nova said simply but gravely, leaving out how he accomplished such a feat. Being in the Mecha City Police didn't give him nearly enough clout to arrange a shuttle to Mars. It was far too hostile a place for anyone to want to go to and getting back to earth once on Mars was even harder. "The authorities made it clear that they weren't going after her. Too risky for one woman."

Marcus wasn't surprised. No one wanted to start another war with Mars, even if Mars was bent on starting one themselves. Not even for someone who had done so much for the community. "You're not coming?" he asked, not missing the fact that Nova had said "you" not "us".

"No." Nova shook his head. "Someone has to stay behind and keep an eye on things, like the company."

"Why not Nebula?"

"She's a busy nurse and I'm still on "sick" leave anyway. Besides, I'd probably just be a liability anyway. Masumi never got to tell me the extent of damage my coding suffered," Nova lamented. It wasn't like he didn't want to go, to save Masumi. He just couldn't.

Marcus looked to the other end of the couch, where he just noticed Rubi and Marin were sitting in utter silence. He was a little more than creeped out at just how invisible they had been to him. "You hear all that? Looks like we're going after all. You ready?"

Rubi nodded slowly, a look of fiery determination in her eyes. "Ready." She turned to face Marin. "You stay. You haven't fully recovered yet."

Marin's ears laid back and she pouted. "But I wanna go home! I wanna help you!"

"Help by staying safe and Mars isn't home. Home is where you're safe, where people don't want to kill you." Rubi was firm. The young badger-therian coming along on a mission was what got them into this position in the first place. She was kidnapped and used to lure Rubi into a trap where she was tormented and brainwashed into working for the Chimera Elite. Rubi could not allow that to happen again, nor allow Marin to be put in such danger again. Rubi had told Miles that she wasn't ready for fieldwork.

"The shuttle won't be ready until tomorrow night, so rest up," Nova spoke up. "And come to terms with the fact that you may never return."

Nova's words weighed heavy, but they were determined. To them, there was no alternative course of action. It was do or die. Marcus could not leave his mother in the claws of those animals to be tortured and killed, and Rubi could not turn her back on her duty to fight the Regime that separated her family.

"I'm going to go pick up some takeout for dinner," Marcus announced, then left the room.

That left Rubi and Marin alone with Nova again. It had still not ceased to be awkward. Rubi knew what she had done to him, though it wasn't under her control. Androids were also featured heavily in Chimera propaganda, portrayed as soulless monsters, which was more accurate to the people orchestrating the lies. Though both the therians knew it was a gross fabrication, it was still hard to shake the horrible images from their minds of the monstrous machines. It didn't help that a long-lost brother of Marcus' had shown up to pick a fight earlier. Rubi was still confused as to why the android had given up so easily, defeated only by words.

It was indeed an uncomfortable situation for Nova as well, though he knew Rubi was only the instrument used; it was really the lynx-therian, Neva, who had killed him. That was who his grudge should be against. Even so, he couldn't force himself to feel hate. This whole situation just left him numb with a vague sense of uneasiness. He knew this was just the beginning, that there may be no end to the troubles that awaited them; even he, who was staying behind on earth, would face trials. He'd have to deal with the reporters, with the questions and accusations. How would he handle it in his state? It didn't seem like his code was seriously damaged, but it wasn't always so easy to tell. Sometimes it took an extra stressful situation to make the break noticeable. The danger that awaited Marcus and Rubi on Mars would undoubtedly be stressful, hence why he was staying behind. It wasn't something he wanted to do, to let Marcus go on alone. Again.

The time passed in absolute silence, everyone brought out of their own deep thoughts by the opening and closing of the front door, footsteps, and Marcus shouting, "I'm back!" He stepped into the room and placed four large, brown paper bags on the coffee table. Nova wordlessly stood up and went to fetch plates and silverware from the kitchen. Marcus opened the bags, pulling out several white takeout containers. He had ordered several different dishes: lo mien, almond chicken, orange chicken, fried rice, and egg drop soup. There were also several egg rolls, rice, and complimentary fortune cookies.

"I wasn't sure what you'd like, so I got several different things," Marcus said to Rubi as he started opening the containers. "I'm sure you'll find something you like."

Rubi stepped over to the coffee table, kneeling in front of it. She sniffed at the contents of the containers, seeming to settle on one. "What's that?"

"Orange chicken," Marcus answered. Nova had returned with the dishes and silverware.

"Looks like chicken nuggets," she observed, recalling the food Nox had brought her earlier.

"Want to try one?" Marcus offered, handing her a fork after she gave a nod. Nova started pouring drinks and handing them out.

Rubi stabbed one of the nuggets which seemed to already have been soaked in something like barbecue sauce, which had also been new to her. Most food she had encountered on earth was. Rubi shoved the whole piece in her mouth and began chewing it. She began chewing it faster and swallowed, then grabbed the closest drink and guzzled down half of it. She panted, only whispering, "Hot."

"A little too much for you, huh?" Marcus laughed, piling on a sizable portion of the spicy stuff on his plate along with some rice. "The rest isn't spicy, I promise. Help yourself. Try a little bit of everything." Though Marcus wasn't aware of the conditions on Mars, he couldn't imagine someone in the Resistance would be able to come by good food such as this.

Rubi did as she was instructed and placed a small portion of each of the other dishes on her plate, as well as a small helping of egg drop soup in a bowl. Though wary from her experience with the orange chicken, she wasn't going to waste an opportunity to eat more than Resistance rations. As Marcus had said, none of the other food turned out to be spicy and the almond chicken was most like the chicken nuggets she had had before; even the almond gravy Marcus suggested to pour on it was good. The lo mien, fried rice, and egg rolls were pleasing as well though not as much. Then it was time to try the egg drop soup. Rubi couldn't remember the last time she had been able to eat an egg. It seemed like forever ago. She had never heard of making soup out of them. Rubi took a small sip from her spoon. After smacking her lips to study the flavor, she quickly finished what was in her bowl.

"Like that, huh?" Marcus poured more into her bowl, which she quickly ate up. "Amazing how something so simple can taste so good."

Rubi finished licking her lips. "Only ruling family and military can get eggs. Rest only get scraps. Most have poor nutrition. Sick, but can't die because of our genes."

It seemed that Rubi was opening up some more. Marcus felt it was a good sign, a sign that she was starting to trust them. They would certainly have to trust each other if they were to complete this mission successfully. Marcus didn't know much at all about the strange kitsune-like therian, but he was confident that he could trust her. Then again, he had thought he could trust Azura as well. Though looking back, he could remember some doubts, but they were rooted in his poor view of himself. Why would such a beautiful, outgoing woman want anything to do with him? It turned out the answer was just information, which did not help how he viewed himself.

"Hey, why the long face?" came a jovial voice. Zeke shortly followed it, Nox coming in behind him.

"Zeke? Nox? What're you doing here?" It wasn't uncommon for them to come over to hang out, but they always texted ahead.

"Nova invited us. Wow, I hope you weren't planning to eat all that by yourself." Zeke planted himself down in front of the coffee table.

"I kind'a was." Well, him and Rubi anyway. It's not that Marcus didn't want to see his friends for possibly the last time, but he hadn't wanted to deal with a tearful

195

goodbye or having Nox deal with the thought of his friend marching off to the nightmare he had escaped and was still tormented by.

"I... remember you," Rubi spoke up. She was looking at Nox.

"Yeah, we met the other day." Nox looked confused.

"No. Years ago. On Mars," Rubi corrected. "The prison."

If a brown-furred bat-therian could look pale, Nox would be doing so right now. "I-I don't remember you." Though, as he spoke those words, something at the back of his mind nagged at him.

Instead of speaking further, Rubi chose to explain in another way. She began to shift to her full therian form, but then started shifting into a red panda instead of a fox.

Nox's eyes widened. "It's y-you! You're the one who caused that commotion to cover our escape. Did you get to earth the same time we did?"

Rubi shook her head. "Wasn't escaping to earth. Only there for a jailbreak."

"Huh?" Nox was more confused.

"She's part of the Resistance on Mars," Marcus interjected.

"Seriously?!" Zeke burst. "Is that why the Chimera Elite are after her?"

Rubi nodded, shifting back into her half-therian form.

"So, they really are an elite squad of fighters? And that's really the Chimera heir?" Zeke asked.

Another nod. They were indeed who they claimed to be.

"Man." Zeke just couldn't believe it. Marcus sure had gotten himself caught up in something big. Though Marcus wasn't just your average guy, being the first and, so far only, techno-organic android on the planet. He was just as fantastic as this whole situation.

They finished the meal in silence, no one being able to come with something say. Even Zeke, who usually always had something to say, was silent. Even Nox, who usually could always find something scientific or technological to babble about, was silent. Even the television was silent, no one bothering to turn it on. It would only be more about Marcus or Masumi, more about what they already knew. This was truly the saddest time they had ever spent together.

CHAPTER 11

Everyone had slept in that morning, not wishing to spend any more time dreading the inevitable than necessary. A few more hours of pretending to have fun wouldn't do any good in the long run. No one was in the mood to pretend anyway.

When everyone finally moseyed out of bed, or the couch, Zeke started cooking breakfast. Rubi silently assisted him. Perhaps, Zeke thought, Marcus could succeed and return. Not only was Marcus clearly built for battle, but he would have the assistance of a member of the Resistance, someone who was used to fighting on Mars. Zeke knew of the horrors there better than most for Nox had shared his experiences when he had finally become comfortable enough to talk about it.

Zeke sat the plates of food out on the table, Rubi setting out silverware and glasses. He had made biscuits and gravy, thinking an especially hearty meal would be helpful to start off the long journey ahead. He sat out the carton of milk and the cartons of juice. Then he called everyone in for breakfast. They all filed in and sat down except for Nova. He remained in the living room, staring at the news broadcast with the closed captioning on so that no one would have to hear it.

They wordlessly dug in, still not having much more to say than the night before. Marcus, Zeke, and Nox didn't need to speak to each other as they all already knew what each other would say. They really were the closest of friends, meeting in high school and sticking together in college.

After breakfast, Marin helped Zeke clean up the table and put the dishes in the dishwasher. She insisted that she was doing better and wanted to help rather than just sit on the couch all day. She didn't want to get weaker while getting better.

Not wanting to just sit around either, Marcus and Rubi engaged in a mock battle in the expanse of the entry room, itching for the real fights to come. They kept use of their elemental abilities to a minimum and were careful not to hit anything around them, practice for avoiding innocent bystanders later. While training, Rubi explained the Chimera Elite's abilities and fighting styles, elaborating on what she shared earlier.

Randor, the leader of the group, usually sent the others on what he considered errands; simple, easy missions he considered too boring for him to bother with. Only when significant threats were involved, like Rubi, did he actually step into the fray. However, he was always training, using the best soldiers in the Chimera military as practice dummies. The heir had been engineered to be the fastest, strongest, toughest therian to ever live, the next step in the bioweapon experiment that spawned the original therians. His most devastating power, however, lied in his sonic scream, an extreme enhancement of a wolf's natural howl. Even the deaf weren't safe from it, as the sound waves would knock one off one's feet. It was his entrance attack and the key to his strategy; knock everyone down and then take them out while dazed. He was truly a devastating hit hard, hit fast force. The citizens of the Chimera Regime had a right to fear him, especially the Resistance and anyone who dared speak out.

"So how do you handle him?" Marcus asked, sending a jab toward Rubi.

"Dodging the sonic blast is the only way. It blows out my flames. You must hit harder and faster than him. Get him talking." Rubi avoided Marcus' fist and sent her own.

Marcus should've guessed. Randor was clearly the egotistical type. It shouldn't be hard to get him monologuing.

Rubi moved on to Azura, Randor's right hand. She had all of Rubi's abilities—pyrokinesis, shapeshifting, levitation—as seen previously. She wasn't a hit hard, hit fast type like Randor, though; she preferred to toy with the enemy as long as possible, only taking them out when it wasn't fun anymore. She was equally difficult to deal with because of her ability to control fire, but she wasn't as easy to trick; she was too much of a trickster herself for that to work.

"I still can't believe I dated her. Let myself think we were dating. Let her use me to get to Mom." Marcus loosely blocked a blow from Rubi, who decided it was time to stop as Marcus' focus had wavered.

"Don't blame yourself. She's very tricky. She's tricked Randor into believing she's loyal," Rubi assured.

"She's not?" Azura sure talked like she was.

"No." Rubi's gaze diverted to the floor. "She's not loyal to anyone."

Marcus was quiet, letting Rubi move on to the others. Neva, as Rubi explained earlier, was the sole survivor of an experiment to unlock telepathy. The procedure had the effect of robbing her of her vision. Had she not have gained telepathy, she would've been tossed away as anything less than perfect was not tolerated by the Chimera Regime. She was used to brainwash people and extract information, later being placed on Randor's team. Jaron was another shapeshifter, though he lacked Rubi and Azura's elemental powers. He was a decent fighter, but not difficult to take down on his own; he was usually sent on recon or to infiltrate. Kyrie could control gravity, which explained why she could knock down Nox and Zeke without touching them. She was also a decent fighter.

"Wow. The Chimera have really been experimenting, haven't they? Couldn't be happy with just being stronger than humans, they had to go for stronger than robots too." Marcus paused. "You think we have a chance of finding my mom alive?"

Rubi nodded. "If they wanted her dead, they wouldn't waste time kidnapping her. They want you. They wouldn't kill their only bait."

Marcus sighed. "Somehow, that's not comforting." Why did they want him? They wouldn't be going through all this trouble for a nobody. They had to know him somehow, know something about him that he didn't. His thoughts went back to that dream of his armored form on Mars, fighting hordes of Chimera. Was it just a dream or had that really happened? Just who was he?

It was time to leave. Marcus had said his quick goodbyes, leaving with Rubi to meet the shuttle's pilot at the rendezvous point. The pilot was a smuggler, a highly paid job for it was also highly dangerous. Anyone, human or therian, caught attempting to smuggle supplies to Mars or smuggle people off Mars, was executed after being tortured as one of the Chimera military researchers' guinea pigs. Usually, they didn't survive to their execution date, killed long before by the inhumane experiments. How Nova managed to make this arrangement was still unanswered, but there were still so many other unanswered questions. If Marcus waited until they were all answered, it would be too late. It was time for action now.

"Jim?" Marcus asked when they arrived at the appointed spot. An older man with a scraggly beard stepped out; he was wearing a pilot's uniform under an old trench coat.

"That's me, kid. You two ready for takeoff?" the old man asked, his voice sounding as ragged as he looked.

Marcus and Rubi both gave a firm nod.

"Alright then. Follow me." The old man led them to the hanger, to the shuttle that was going to take them to the red planet. It was a fairly small shuttle, no bigger than a bus. Anything bigger would be too easily caught.

They followed the old man in, who sat down in the pilot's chair. Marcus and Rubi sat in the seats behind him, strapping themselves in. It wasn't too long before they were cleared, and the shuttle took off into the sky. It was smooth sailing for a while until they hit the upper atmosphere. Before they knew it, they were in space. Marcus looked out the window, marveling at all the stars. He could get lost just staring at them, losing himself in the vastness of space. Various facts from his astronomy classes came to him, but he didn't share.

His daydreaming was interrupted by the sound of someone vomiting. Marcus stuck his tongue out and Rubi cringed at the sound. Knowing it wasn't the pilot, Marcus shouted, "Who's there?"

"I told you you'd get space sick! I told you to take the motion sickness pills! But did you listen? No, of course not!" It was Nox's voice.

"Just shut up and get a mop!" Zeke's voice. "You only have to smell it! I have to taste it!"

Marcus stood up and stepped to the back of the shuttle's passenger section. Zeke, Nox, and Marin were in the back seat. "What are you three doing here?!"

"Well, you see-" Nox began, stroking one of his massive ears.

"It was his idea!" Zeke pointed at Nox.

"What? No, it wasn't. It was a... mutually agreed upon..." he trailed off.

Marin was quietly cleaning up the vomit with some supplies she found, not wanting her nose to be assaulted by the awful smell. Rubi walked back there and gave the badger-therian a disapproving look. The girl was an orphan and Rubi had hoped to leave her back on earth where she'd have a better life, get to grow up, and grow old.

"Okay, next question: how?" Nova had to make special arrangements to get just Marcus and Rubi on the shuttle.

"Nox is a master hacker and you ask how?" Zeke mused.

"I'm not a hacker," Nox corrected. "I'm a computer science major. There's a difference."

"Sure," Zeke grinned, not at all believing him.

Marcus' planted his face firmly in his palm. They were arguing over trivialities when they were in space on their way to the most dangerous place in the solar system. Well, other than the inhospitable planets and the sun itself.

"Seriously, why are you here? I'd think of all people, you two would be the last to want to come. You barely escaped Mars the first time, Nox, and Zeke, you've been afraid of space ever since that field trip on the space station where you almost died! I just don't get it!" Marcus seemed about to lose it.

"Why do you think I threw up?" Zeke half-heartedly chuckled, flexing the fingers of his bionic arm. "Look, mate, you're our best friend."

"Only friend," Nox corrected.

Zeke glanced at Nox before continuing. "We've always had each other's backs. We're in this together, wherever it ends."

Marcus sighed, then smiled. "Thanks, guys." He chuckled. "Your dad's gonna be so mad when he finds out."

Zeke just shrugged. "He'll get over it."

"So, how did you plan on fighting? They're not exactly schoolyard bullies." Marcus finally sat down.

"Nox took care of that." Zeke stood up and tapped the top of what looked like a watch that was on his wrist. A suit of armor appeared on him. It was muted oranges and browns, with a helmet and visor. The armor plates looked heavy like they could take a beating. "He snuck into the lab and whipped up some cool armor suits based on your mum's notes."

"Yes, well, I had to make some modifications, so they'd work on fully organic lifeforms, but..." Nox stood up and activated his armor. It was far lighter weight and in grays and blacks, made more for stealth. "They should work well enough."

It was Marin's turn to stand up and activate her armor. Hers was purple and was in between Zeke's and Nox's reinforcement wise. "I can help now. I can be strong like you!" she declared.

Rubi gave her a tired stare, then sighed while closing her eyes. She reached out and pated Marin on the head. There was no stopping her and no convincing her that her hero wasn't that strong. Rubi had never felt that she was strong, only a scared child trying to survive. The only thing she felt was tired; it was the only thing she could feel anymore. She couldn't allow empathy for the Chimera's victims anymore for it would overwhelm her and then she wouldn't be able to do her job of protecting them, which even now she was failing at. She had to go off-world and find a powerful battle android of legend to succeed where she failed. Maybe he could be the hero they thought she was.

"Hey, Marcus," Nox interrupted the silence. "I brought your tablet too. I thought it'd be a good idea to go through your coding and see if there's anything else that hasn't been unlocked yet, like how your armor was, that would be useful."

"Yeah, I guess it would be better to go in with as many cards as possible." Marcus pulled off his jacket and shirt, then unscrewed the circular part in the middle of his chest that protected his USB ports. Nox handed him a cord, the other end already plugged into the android's personal tablet, which had a special app developed by Masumi. It could run diagnostics and edit coding, but the latter was almost completely locked down so that only Masumi could change anything. Marcus assumed that Nox had already found a way to work past that, likely using something he found in the lab.

Nox scrolled down the screen of mind-numbingly complex code. Few people would be able to make sense of it. Valroids were still arguably the most advanced androids on the planet. No one had been able to do better than the Valkos so far. It took Nox some time to get familiar with the code's structure. "Ah, I think I found something. It looks like it was locked on purpose rather than the data being fragmented. Let's see what this does. Run program," Nox mumbled.

"That's doesn't sound promis-" Marcus started but promptly stopped as he felt his body changing. It felt different than transforming into his armor as that formed on top of his body. This felt like it was changing his body, altering the properties of the nanites that it was made up of. First, his skin turned charcoal gray, then his skin turned into fur. His ears shifted to the top of his head and became triangular, his nose elongated into a snout, his nails changed into claws, and a tail sprouted. Marcus looked down at himself, blinking. "Um, what is this? Nox...?"

"I don't know," Nox admitted, frantically looking through the code. "There's no indicator. Maybe it was a disguise. If you were sent to Mars during the war, you would've needed one." Nox closed out the program, pulling the cord from Marcus, who screwed the cap back into his chest. Once in, it promptly changed to match the rest of him, blending in because of the fur.

"I guess so," Marcus agreed. "Just how many secrets has mom been keeping from me? Not that it matters now. We've got a job to do." Marcus clenched his fists and transformed into his armor to test if anything had changed with the therian disguise. His armor's appearance had altered to match his wolf form. The red sections became black and the gold sections became red. He also had a metal tail and his helmet now had a wolf ear design.

"Wow, even your armor's different. Masumi really thinks of everything," Zeke remarked.

"Yeah…" Marcus switched out of his armor. He slipped his shirt and jacket back on, then sat down. "I guess this form could come in handy. Too bad we don't have a disguise for you."

CHAPTER 12

The rest of the trip was uneventful with little chatter. They were all preparing for the fight to come. Only Rubi was really certain of what may await, of the true danger lying ahead. She knew Marcus was up to it but was unsure about the others. To her knowledge, they were not warriors. Nox had escaped Mars before; would his fear of this place keep him from fighting? Zeke had a bionic limb, but it wasn't made for combat; could he handle the fight ahead? And what of Marin? Rubi knew she had fight in her and was eager to prove herself, but she was still young and inexperienced. They all had armor to protect themselves with and enhance their strength, but it would take more than that to defeat the Chimera Elite and the Chimera military, which would undoubtedly be sent after them.

The shuttle sat down in a deep canyon to avoid detection, having evaded the satellites by using the latest in cloaking technology. It was expensive but in this line of work, incredibly worth it. If an unauthorized craft were detected by Martian satellites, it'd be shot down with missiles without warning or an attempt to discover who was on board. To say the Chimera were heartless was an understatement.

This canyon had a secret entrance to one of the resistance's many bases. Moving underground was the only safe way. Rubi led the others off the shuttle and to this base. It was a small one, only for ferrying people to shuttles hidden in the canyon to smuggle them off-world. There were boxes of supplies, which Rubi quickly dug into. She pulled out cloaks and handed them to each of them, putting one on herself.

"What are these?" Marcus asked. "Besides cloaks."

"Special cloaks. The fabric changes color to blend into the environment." Rubi pulled the hood over her head. The cloak's color changed to match the colors of the base around her.

"Hey, I can still see you," Zeke pointed out. "You're not invisible."

"Didn't say invisible. Doesn't work well close up, only far away."

"Oh, okay." Zeke put his cloak on.

"Have to rendezvous with the resistance. They can find your mother. Follow me and pay attention. Anything can happen." Rubi walked off, heading deeper into the cave. Marcus began to follow her, then Marin, then Zeke, then Nox. The bat's ears twitched in all directions, listening for the smallest sound. The group marched on through the cave system. Marcus wondered if it was natural or had been dug out. There was so much about Mars that scientists on earth just didn't know since no one was allowed to come here and any satellites or rovers sent to collect data were quickly destroyed. The governments of earth also discouraged anyone from sending information gathering equipment so as not to start another war with the Chimera.

"Someone's ahead," Nox spoke up from the back. "Multiple people."

Rubi gave a single nod to acknowledge his warning but continued. The hallway opened up into a room, the group stopping at the entrance. Inside were Chimera soldiers dressed in their rusty uniforms and holding plasma blasters. Opposite them was a lone gerbil-therian in an outfit matching Rubi's.

"Miles." Rubi dashed off into the room, taking fire from Miles. She was catching the plasma bolts and forming them into a ball with her hand, the ball growing with each bolt fired. Rubi sent the plasma back at them in a wide blast. The soldiers screamed, several running off down the different tunnels. Marcus jumped into the room, firing electric blasts and the remaining ones, which quickly decided to join the others in their escape. Shortly, the base was free of soldiers. Miles ran up to Rubi.

"Rubi, thank goodness! I thought the Chimera Elite would've killed you for sure." Miles looked ragged, his clothes torn and patches of fur missing.

"Where are the others?" she asked.

"They're gone, every last one of them! The military hunted us down, got everyone but me, even the children! There's no one left."

Rubi's face turned dark. The entire resistance—except for her, Miles, and Marin —gone? It was as she feared. They were destroyed in her absence. She had been the only one keeping them from extinction.

Tears welled up in her eyes and streamed down her face. She collapsed to her hands and knees, sobbing. The others glanced at each other, shifting uncomfortably.

Marcus knelt in front of Rubi. "I know you're upset, but it's not safe to stay here. We need to leave now. Once we find my mother, we'll make them pay, I promise you. We'll make them pay for all the innocents they took."

Rubi sniffled, then stood up. She couldn't waste time mourning; she couldn't let their deaths go unpunished. Now Marcus really was their last hope, their last hope for Mars and maybe the system; maybe beyond.

"This way." Miles took over leading the party to their next destination. Rubi followed alongside Marcus, trying to dry her eyes, and preparing herself for the next battle, which could be at any time. The

Chimera military probably knew the whole system of resistance tunnels by now. No place would be safe to hide.

"There's something I should tell you," Rubi said to Marcus, her voice shaky.

"You don't have to talk now," he assured.

"No. I must tell you what I know, what I've known this whole time," Rubi insisted.

"What're you talking about?" Marcus questioned, confusion and apprehension written on his face.

"I know what you are. I found you in an abandoned underground lab here, on this planet, five years ago. You were in a stasis tube."

"A... stasis tube? Here? How?" Marcus thought back to his dream again; of being on Mars in this armor. I guess it wasn't a dream.

"My father had found you collapsed, near death, twenty years ago, at the end of Beast War. He took you to a secret lab and put you in stasis to preserve your organic parts," she elaborated. "I found the lab five years ago. I released you, but you attacked me, fighting like a mindless beast. I stopped you and took you to the resistance, who smuggled you to earth to Valko Industries."

Marcus was in shock. The pieces were finally fitting together, the puzzle was becoming clear. That dream had been a memory of him fighting on Mars in the Beast War as one of the battle androids that were made stronger than the therians. He had been built for that purpose, but why had his mother kept it secret and why had he lost his memories? Was Magneto right about her? Did she really erase his memories? Or did his damage in battle remove them?

"If you knew all along, then why didn't ya tell him until now?" Zeke demanded in an accusatory tone. By this time, the group had stopped moving forward.

Rubi swallowed hard. "Didn't know if I could trust him. I may have stopped him five years ago, but... I was severely wounded. Took months to heal. Resistance lost many battles in that time. Couldn't risk it."

"I understand," Marcus admitted.

"That's it? She kept secrets from you and it's all good?" Zeke didn't want to let it go so easily.

"You just heard her reasons," Marcus stated, "and Mom kept secrets too, but I'm here to rescue her anyway. Besides, you and Nox kept that you found Rubi a secret for a while. There's more at stake here than our personal feelings. This is bigger than any of us. This could be... war."

Zeke grew silent but was still resentful to the situation. It was bad enough that his best friend's girlfriend turned out to be a spy. He knew Marcus was just keeping his feelings sealed away, acting like he wasn't affected.

"Only after going through the lab and my father's notes, did I realize what you were, who you were. I knew I had to get you back, to get your help," Rubi admitted.

"Wait, you came to find me? You mean, this was all a-"

"You mean you got kidnapped on purpose?" Miles questioned, cutting off Marcus.

"Yes. I knew it was a trap, but I knew where they were going and knew it was the only way to get to earth and to you since the Elite was looking for you too," she confirmed.

"But why? Why were the Elite looking for me? To get to my mother? How did they know about the armor?" Despite all the answers, Marcus still had a million questions.

"I... don't know," Rubi replied.

"A likely story," Zeke commented, folding his arms.

"This isn't the time, Zeke," Nox finally spoke up. His movements were twitchy, like a meerkat on the lookout for lions. "We have to trust her. I trust her. She's the one who helped break me and my mother out Chimera prison. We're on the same side."

The group was silent. Their hearts weighed heavy with the revelations and realizations of the situation. They wordlessly continued their journey until Rubi broke the silence.

"The resistance may have seen me as their secret weapon but, I was only barely able to keep them alive. I'm only one and the Elite are five. Now we are six, and one of us is the legendary hero of the Beast War."

"Legendary hero..." Marcus whispered. He was not at all used to the idea. If only he could remember more. Would he be able to fight as well as before? "Wait, is that why you attacked me before? You assumed I was hostile?"

"Yes."

After several hours of traveling through the tunnels, the group stopped to rest. It would do no good to run into more soldiers if they were too weary to fight. Rubi found a corner to curl up into and fell asleep almost instantly, worn out from the trek and the emotional exhaustion. Marin curled up beside her, falling asleep just as easily. Zeke deactivated his armor and used his cloak as a blanket, laying down. Nox left his armor on and flew up to the ceiling, affixing his boots so that he could sleep upside down; his wings hugged his body. Miles sat down, silently deciding that he'd take first watch. Marcus sat down beside him.

"Maybe you can answer some of my questions. I'd rather not bother Rubi anymore. She's lost more than I have." Currently, that he knew of, anyway. He didn't know what he may have lost as Dynamo, not that it made a difference now, as he didn't remember.

"I can try." Miles was wearier than all of them and nervous. He remembered how

Rubi looked after her first meeting with the android. It was a sight he'd not soon forget.

"She said the resistance considered her their secret weapon. It's obvious why. She has some form of pyrokinesis which, apparently, also means manipulating plasma. She can also shapeshift. What I don't understand is how she can do these things. I know the Chimera did experiments resulting in one of the Elite getting telepathy, but Rubi's powers are next level." They were on par with his but seemed even more fantastic. He understood the mechanisms behind his abilities, but not hers.

"We're not sure," Miles admitted. "Our only guess was she's the result of some radical military experiments to create a more powerful bioweapon. Most of their other experiments just resulted in extreme enhancements to natural abilities, things that were already there. Like a wolf's howl turning into Randor's sonic scream. We don't know how they got Rubi and Azura to create and control fire or to shapeshift."

"Maybe the shapeshifting came from octopus DNA," Marcus suggested, "but that wouldn't account for the pyrokinesis or flight. Could they have come up with something new? Something not already in the animal kingdom?"

"I don't know but that's not all they did to Rubi. Her..." Miles looked down at his palms. "...blood is even different." His fingers slowly curled inward, making fists.

"How do you mean?"

"You haven't noticed? Take another look at her skin, at her lips. Don't you think it's a bit odd just how much of an orange hue her skin has, just how orange her lips are?" Miles posed.

"I guess? I mean, maybe she's just bad at approximating human skin tones. Look, I've been distracted by more important things, like the Chimera trying to kill me and kidnap my mom," Marcus defended. He was normally good at picking up on details, but this one hadn't seemed important enough to note.

"No, that's not it at all. Her blood is orange! More than that, she's somehow able to breathe hydrogen as well as oxygen, and she has to avoid too much sunlight. Once, she got lost on the surface and it was days before we found her. When we did, her blood had turned green! She was green! We had no idea what to do for her. All we could do was bring her back to base and try to keep her stable. After a few days, her color went back to normal. When we asked her about it, all she said was 'sunlight'. So, ever since, we avoided sending her to the surface during the day."

Marcus looked over at Rubi, realizing just how strange she was. Azura didn't have the same hue to her skin, so Marcus assumed her blood was normal. Rubi must've been experimented on beyond Azura. Maybe that's why the Elite were after her. Rubi was meant to join their team, but she refused.

"The kitsune's real quiet, doesn't say much. We do know that her father was originally a military researcher and that the jumpsuit she wears was engineered by him to help protect her blood from the sun's rays. It got all torn up in the fight before she got lost. That's why she got sick. That thing's been patched up so many times, same as her. The kitsune's quiet, but she's a good kid. Always risking herself to protect others, even postponed looking for her father to join us. I just wish we could've come through on our end to find him for her." Miles looked somber. He had lost everything too, same as Rubi. Maybe it was worse for him because he was here when it happened but still could do nothing. Rubi had the excuse of being off world, dealing with another set of problems.

"Maybe we still can when this is all over. She's helping me rescue my mom, it's the least I could do in return." Marcus held a hand in front of his face.

Miles smiled, a weary smile, but a smile. "The resistance has passed down stories of you for two decades, stories of Dynamo. You're... not a disappointment." Tears streamed down his face. "I had lost hope, but now... I know we can win this."

Marcus closed his eyes. He had not planned on coming here to fight a war with the Chimera, but it seemed that it was inevitable. They had started it by kidnapping his mother. Besides, what was left for him on earth? Nova and Nebula were tough, they didn't need him. His friends were here with him and his mother was awaiting rescue. Marcus' only focus was completing this mission, wherever it may take him. There was no way back.

"Yeah, no problem." A smug grin spread on Marcus' face. "I already did it once, so I should be able to do it again, right?" Marcus yawned. "After I rest."

"You... need to rest?" Miles raised a brow.

"Oh, yeah, all androids need to rest. Most just need to reboot like a computer, but I need to sleep." Marcus stretched out on the ground, covering himself with his cloak. "I'm the first, and still only, techno-organic robot."

"Amazing. You and Rubi are really alike. Both unique, one of a kind," Miles commented.

"Yeah, I guess so." Marcus yawned again. "Wake me for the next watch, okay? You may have to punch me awake, I'm a heavy sleeper," he chuckled.

"Alright," Miles agreed, though he hoped to not have to resort to such drastic methods. It's not that he thought he could hurt the android, but he didn't want the android attacking him in a defensive reaction. He knew what Marcus was capable of and that was probably just a fraction of his power.

Azura was gazing out the window, but not looking at anything. She was lost in her thoughts, thinking back to when this mission began, to when she first met Marcus. Dynamo's location had been narrowed down to Mecha City, but Azura had had a difficult time turning up any leads. There was simply no data to be found on the enemy of the Chimera Regime as if he had been erased. Frustrated with the dead ends, Azura—in her fully human disguise—had sat down on the curb in front of an ice cream shop. How was she going to explain her failure to Randor? She wasn't a researcher or a detective. That's when Marcus had come by.

"Hey, you okay?" he had asked. Marcus had been holding an ice cream cone in his hand; chocolate with brownie bits in a waffle cone. He had the most innocent expression.

Azura had looked startled but quickly regained her composure. "Oh, I-" She came up with a story and quickly. Someone had happened to be passing by wearing a college jacket. "I was just looking for campus. I'm planning to start in the fall, so I wanted to scope it out, but I don't seem to be having any luck finding it. My phone's GPS is on the fritz and I'm just no good with maps."

"Really? I go to Mecha City University too. I just finished my first year. I can take you there and show you around if you want," Marcus had offered.

"Oh, that's sweet of you, you don't have to do that." Azura had not wanted to tour campus but outright refusing might be suspicious.

"No, it's fine. I've nothing better to do. Except eat ice cream," he had chuckled.

Azura had laughed with him.

"Hey, how about I buy you an ice cream, then we can leave when we're done? I can't exactly drive holding a cone. Well, I can, but it's not... advisable."

"Oh, I couldn't." She had wondered how this guy could be so nice to a stranger. "You don't even know me."

"So? I didn't use to know my best friends either. It's no big deal. I've plenty of money," Marcus had assured.

"Oh? And how does a college student have so much money?" Azura had posed.

"Well, it's actually Mom's money, but she doesn't mind. It's not like she could spend it all herself. See, she's the CEO Valko Industries," Marcus had explained.

"Masumi Valko is your mother? I didn't know she had human children." This time, Azura's surprise had been genuine.

"Oh, I'm not human. I'm an android, the first and only techno-organic android," Marcus had half-bragged.

"I never would have guessed. Your mom must've done a good job." Azura had gone back to acting.

"Sure did. Now, how about we get you that ice cream, then we can head out when we're done. You don't mind riding on a magcycle, do you?" Marcus had asked.

"Certainly not." Azura had followed Marcus back into the ice cream shop to get her cone. Marcus had paid as promised. They had sat outside to eat their cones and chat about college. Marcus had shared that he was majoring in astronomy. Azura had to come up with a major, having told him that she was going to major in fashion design. After having finished their ice cream, the two had hopped on Marcus' magcycle and took off for Mecha City campus. It hadn't been long after that that the two began dating. To actually get into college, she had to have Neva brainwash some people to get Azura a forged birth certificate, a state ID, and into college. It hadn't taken long—a little over a semester—for Azura to figure out that Marcus was actually Dynamo with his memories and ability to transform missing. After that, she had gone to work on making him remember, enlisting Neva's help in jogging his memory.

"I just don't see the point in waiting until Dynamo gets his memories back. Why give him the chance to defeat us?" Azura complained. "Take him out now before he becomes more of a threat."

You can't fool me. Neva approached, making her presence known, speaking to

Azura's mind directly. I know what your feelings are.

"Don't be foolish," Azura snarled. "I was only pretending to date him to get information on Dynamo, who he happened to be. I don't care about him any more than I care about you."

"Or your sister?"

Azura swiftly spun around, kicking Neva across the room and into the wall. The blue fox-therian charged after her. Neva held up her hand and Azura froze in place. Her muscles twitched, trying to break free, but she couldn't.

Randor wouldn't like it if you killed me, a one-of-a-kind weapon, Neva warned. The researchers still haven't been able to duplicate my powers successfully.

Azura hissed. "Randor may not always protect you. When that day comes, I will kill you."

Neva stood up, releasing Azura's body from her mental grip. I know.

Reaching into her pocket, Azura pulled out a small remote. She pressed a button and Neva let out a scream, collapsing to the ground in agony. The computerized collar around her neck and the bracelets and anklets around her wrists and ankles glowed and crackled with electricity. Azura hit the button again, ending Neva's torture. The blue fox-therian left, leaving the lynx-therian to recover from the pain and reflect on her actions.

In a nearby room, Randor sat nonchalantly in a chair like it was his throne although it was little more than an office chair, a prideful grin on his face. "So, you've finally come to your senses, hmm? You've finally admitted to the foolishness of your little rebellion and come to surrender?"

The person he spoke to, who stood across from him with head hung low, nodded. "The resistance is dead, and I'll only end up with them if I don't surrender. Just... please don't hurt Rubi," he pleaded, clenching his fists and fighting back tears.

"It was never my intention to kill her," Randor assured, leaning an elbow on the arm of his chair, and resting his head on his fist. "It would be a waste to destroy such a unique specimen such as her. No, my intention was always to get her to join us, just like her sister."

Miles' eyes narrowed. "You know that Rubi isn't like Azura. She'll never join you willingly. She'd die first."

"Trust me, I know." Randor stroked his chin. He stood up and paced away from Miles. "That is why you'll be leading them all into a trap. I wanted to wait until Dynamo was ready but... my father's put pressure on me. He wants results." Randor stepped over to Miles and held out a key card. "You will take this. It will allow you access to the head research facility and all the rooms inside. You can tell them you stole it." Randor dropped the card into Miles' open palms. "Just get them there. My team will do the rest."

Miles stared at the key card. The feel of it in his palms was like acid as if it threatened to burn a hole through his hands. His chest grew cold.

"What's the matter?" Randor questioned in a mocking tone. "You can't be having second thoughts now. Did you think that the resistance leader could surrender without having to pay a price or deal with consequences?"

Miles gripped the card tight in his hand, his fearful face turning serious. He still felt anxious but also felt resolve. He knew he had to do this. They had lost the fight, it was over. It was time for the suffering to end. He just hoped that Rubi would understand.

"Now go. The longer you're away, the more likely they are to question your absence." Randor returned to his chair. "And don't mess this up."

"Yes, sir," Miles acknowledged. He turned to leave, not wanting to be here any longer than necessary. His stomach was in a knot and he felt like he would be sick. He had to get it under control, or the others would suspect something. For that matter, he had to get back before anyone woke up. Hopefully, Marcus was as heavy a sleeper as he claimed.

When he made it back, he found everyone in the same place as they were when he had left. All of them were still fast asleep, undisturbed by his absence. He crept over to Rubi, watching her even breaths. Just by looking at her now, no one would be able to guess that she was a member of the former resistance or that she had taken down so many Chimera soldiers. "You won't have to fight anymore," Miles whispered, his voice barely audible.

Rubi stirred, but simply rolled over and curled into an even tighter ball than before. After breathing a soft sigh of relief, Miles returned to the spot he had been before. He would wait about an hour more before waking up Marcus for his shift. Miles needed

time to compose himself before facing
anyone.

CHAPTER 13

The next morning, Miles continued to lead the team through the tunnel system. They avoided soldiers when they could, taking them head-on when they couldn't. Marcus and Rubi were always on the forefront, charging off before anyone else could react, like trained soldiers themselves.

The others only handled the ones that managed to get past the two.

"They sure fight good together," Zeke remarked.

"Yeah, I guess they do," Nox agreed.

When they finally made it to their destination, it felt like they had spent an eternity in those tunnels. The group stepped out into the light; sunlight that had been redirected with mirrors to illuminate the underground city. Despite being beneath the surface, it looked like a fairly normal city with buildings, roads, transports driving by, and people.

Rubi pulled her hood down farther to shield her eyes from the light. She also shifted her form to appear full therian. Zeke also kept his hood down to hide the fact that he was not a therian at all, though he wondered if he would get sniffed out.

Marcus changed into his wolf-therian disguise, not as concerned about covering his face. Maybe they should have worked on disguises, but there hadn't been time to fully coordinate. Zeke, Nox, and Marin's presence hadn't even been planned. Could they even win with such a poorly thought-out plan? Maybe it wasn't as poorly thought out as it was very barebones. The idea was to find where Masumi was being kept and to, essentially, storm the castle. A very heads-on approach but what chance did they have of sneaking in? It would probably be a highly secure location, a veritable stronghold. Maybe they could do like when they rescued Marin; have Marcus and Rubi create a diversion while the others snuck past to free Masumi. Nox might be able to handle the security system, but there were so many ways it could go wrong.

They stepped into the crowd, sticking out more in their attempt to blend in. Marcus noticed that most of the people there weren't wearing cloaks, making him feel like he had a neon sign floating above his head warning the others of his alien presence. Stealing quick glances at the therian's eyes, almost all of them seemed to be purposefully diverting their gaze, like they didn't want to address the elephant in the room. Perhaps being obvious would work to their advantage. No one was bothering them so far, in any case. Shifting his focus to his surroundings rather than the people, Marcus noticed small stands lining the roads which held a variety of goods, including food. It seemed to be a farmer's market, which struck Marcus as odd. He never imagined that the oppressive Chimera Regime would allow such a freedom as to sell one's own goods. He suspected high taxes were in place so that the government reaped most of what the people had sown. It occurred to him that no on earth—except for those who had escaped from Mars—knew what life was really like here. The Chimera government saw to that, making sure no information got out or in. The people here didn't know what life was like on earth either. The two worlds were completely cut off from each other, only vaguely aware of the other's existence.

Marcus was torn from his thoughts by a shout. He and the others quickly turned in the voice's direction. A couple of Chimera soldiers were laughing at an old man, poking at him with their blasters' barrels.

"What a couple 'o jerks," Zeke spat.

It was wordlessly, unanimously decided that it would be better to not get involved.

Causing a commotion would blow their cover and compromise their mission. It wasn't something that any of them were happy with, but they knew how serious this was. They continued, pretending to ignore the spectacle.

That is, until one of the soldiers struck the old man with the butt of his blaster and blood trickled down the side of his head. Marcus dashed forward without a second's thought, weaving through the crowd. He thrust a fist into the soldier's face, knocking him off his feet.

"Hey!" the grounded soldier's buddy shouted. "Striking a soldier is punishable by death!" He aimed his blaster at Marcus, firing it.

Marcus dodged, the blast piercing through his cloak and scorching a stand. He dashed forward, grabbing the soldier's blaster, and pointing it upward before he fired, the blast hitting the high ceiling. Marcus ripped the blaster from the soldier's hand and hit him across the face with it, dropping him next to his buddy.

"I think I'll be keeping this." Marcus looked over the blaster in his hands. It would be useful. His electricity only had so much reach and he was unable to generate it when not in his armor.

"You won't want to be doing that, sir." The old man said from his spot on the ground. He was sitting up, a hand on his head.

"Why not?"

"Don't you know? All military weapons have GPS trackers in them. As soon as you deviate from these soldiers' planned path, a squadron will be sent to hunt you down."

"Ah, right, of course." Marcus hadn't known that but had to pretend to. Instead of just tossing the blaster away, however, he ripped it apart with his bare hands. He might have been in his civilian mode—albeit in therian disguise—but he had quite a bit of strength without his armor. Marcus picked up the other blaster and did the same to it. Then he turned to the old man. "Are you alright?"

"Yeah, I'll be okay, but I fear this will not go unnoticed. Even without the tracker, they will still hunt you down. An old man like me wasn't worth it."

"Everyone's worth it," Marcus stated as the rest of the group showed up.

The old man forced himself to his feet and grabbed some bags, handing them to Marcus and each of his friends. "Here. Here. Take as much of my produce as you would like."

"Oh, no, that's not neces-" Marcus started but was promptly cut off.

"No, I insist. It's very necessary." The old man gestured enthusiastically to his stand. "Now, collect your reward and hurry. It won't be long before your handiwork is discovered."

"Thank you," Marcus accepted. The others had already begun filling their bags, seeing no point in arguing against free food.

"You're a funny boy," the old man remarked. "Thanking me when you're the one who saved my life!" He chuckled. "Oh, but we could use more like you, boy. Say, what's your name?"

Marcus hesitated, unsure of how to answer. Giving this man his real name would do no real harm, but he wondered if he should give him his other, old name. This man was obviously no supporter of the current regime, but could he afford to give people hope when there was a good chance that they would fail this mission? "It's... Dynamo," he finally answered.

"Dynamo?" The old man's eyes widened. "So, you were named after him? He came... he came real close to freeing us."

"No, I wasn't named after him," Marcus corrected, looking him straight in the eyes. "I am him."

The old man's eyes opened even wider. "No... no way!" he whispered. "Those... those red eyes! It is you!" He chuckled. "I guess that's twice you've saved my life, ha, what a small world! ...worlds? Oh, well. You should get going, I'm sure you have a very important mission. Have you returned to finish what you started?"

Marcus hesitated again. Could he make that promise? He had only come for his mother, but it looked like he wasn't going to be able to get away with just that. The Elite wouldn't let him, not to mention the military. It looked like his course of action was determined for him. "Yes."

"Splendid! Thank you, for giving an old man hope. Now, go, before I gab on and they catch you." He jovially shooed Marcus and his friends away.

"Right, let's go guys." Marcus led them away, continuing further into the city. He hoped there were no more soldiers wandering around as completing their mission would quickly become difficult, if not impossible. At least meeting that old man gave Marcus hope about the state of things. Maybe earth wouldn't have to worry about the Chimera if the current regime were toppled. It was strange to think he had met the man twenty years ago when over a week ago he had still believed he had only been created five years ago.

Miles resumed leading the group as Marcus had no idea where they were or where they were going, and Rubi didn't seem to have it in her to lead anyone anywhere right now. They traversed through more of the city, which had more of the same. Marcus wondered if they were all like this. Miles stopped as they came to a train station.

"We'll need to take a train to get to the capital quick enough, which is the most likely place they'll have your mother," Miles whispered. "It won't be easy."

"I was afraid you'd say that," Marcus sighed. "And I'm afraid to ask but, why won't It be easy?"

"To get on the train, you need to show your ID," Miles explained.

"Which none of us have." Marcus stroked his chin, wondering how to get around this. The Chimera Regime really wanted to know what its citizens were up to, it seemed. It would certainly keep their enemies from traveling freely. That was probably why the resistance had secret tunnels, which were not so secret anymore. If only they had been able to get here sooner.

"There's a guy nearby who sells fake IDs," Miles shared, keeping his voice extremely low and his face close to the others.

"Ah, but we don't have any money." Not on him, anyway. Back on earth, Marcus could access his mother's large funds, but here? He was penniless. Though, he doubted a man in the Martian black market would take earth credit cards or even earth dollars.

"He may be willing to trade," Miles admitted. "We can find him and ask, at least. Traveling on foot would take too long and risk too many encounters with the military."

"Alright, let's go." Marcus didn't want to take a detour, but this seemed the only way to get to where his mother most likely was. Hopefully, this man Miles knew would cooperate.

Miles turned and walked off into the crowd, the others following behind him. He stopped at a symbol drawn on a pillar that had been made with near the same color paint as the pillar itself, only noticeable to someone looking for it. Miles led them to several more of these painted symbols, some on walls, some on floors, some on other structures. Finally, Miles seemed to find the place he was looking for. There were large metal crates stacked up in front of a doorway with just enough room for someone to slip through. Miles led them through into a hallway and down a flight of stairs to a dark room filled with junk.

A monkey-therian stepped out from the shadows. His clothes were worn, and he didn't seem like he had been eating enough. "What do you lot want? Who are you? More soldiers? What else can you take from me?"

"We're not soldiers," Marcus corrected, growing uneasy.

"We're... what's left of the resistance," Miles admitted. "We need fake IDs to get on the train and get to the capital."

"The capital? What do you want to go there for? To get the rest of you killed?" The monkey-therian's gaze settled on the others. "You guys don't look like resistance."

Miles was about to respond, but Marcus cut in. "We're not, except for him and her." He pointed to Miles and then Rubi. "The rest of us... are from earth. The Chimera Elite kidnapped my mother and we're here to rescue her."

At first, the monkey-therian didn't know what to say. "Earth?!" It seemed incredulous to him. "Why would the Chimera Elite kidnap your mother?! And what would you be doing here to get her back?! You even know who the Elite are?!"

"Yes, we've fought them," Marcus answered, trying to keep his cool. Try as he might, he was unable to keep the snarl out of his voice. "My mother is Masumi Valko, owner of Valko Industries, partially responsible for the Valroids that fought the

Chimera during the war. Her husband was killed by Chimera when the war started." It was certainly not a stretch to see why his mother would be targeted by the Chimera Elite. The bigger question would be why they didn't go after her sooner. Could they have been waiting for Dynamo's reappearance?

"Oh, well then, I guess that makes a little more sense," the monkey-therian admitted. "Not that much makes sense anymore. Local government leader gets wind of my black-market dealings, but has my wife and son arrested instead, leaving me free."

"That's awful!" Zeke exclaimed.

"They don't care about enforcing the law," Rubi spoke, "only controlling the people through fear. We may be willing to risk ourselves, but not our loved ones."

"The little lady's right. I'm afraid the people haven't much fight left in them, especially with the news of the resistance being crushed. How did you two survive?" the monkey-therian asked.

"Luck on my part," Miles answered. "I was on a solo mission when it happened. Rubi had been kidnapped prior by the Chimera Elite and taken to earth. They had Neva brainwash her and used her as a pawn until Marcus here got involved."

The therian-monkey stroked his chin. "Rubi, hmm?" He squinted at her. "Yes, you are the resistance's little secret weapon." He mumbled to himself, looking through some things on his cluttered desk. "Fake IDs to get on the train you say? Very well. It'll take time. Time enough for you to rescue my wife and son."

"Agreed," Marcus said without hesitation.

"Hold on," Zeke interjected. "We don't even know where they are, and we could get captured before even getting to your mum."

"But we need those IDs, Zeke, and that's the price." Marcus folded his arms. "We knew this wasn't going to be easy."

"Yeah, yeah, I just didn't think we'd have to go through so many hoops," Zeke grumbled. Although on a planet, he still considered himself as being in space and wasn't happy about it.

"You can't always just storm the castle, you know. Sometimes there are side quests you have to take care of first. Think of this as one of those." Marcus turned to leave and lead the group out. "Besides, this place isn't any more dangerous than where you grew up. Spiders, snakes, murderous birds..."

"I guess you're right about that," Zeke relented with a laugh.

"Remind me to never let you take me there for vacation ever again." Marcus cringed at the thought of having to deal with all those creatures as he peered around the boxes to check if anyone was watching. Satisfied that no one was, he stepped out from behind them and waved the others on.

"Now where's your sense of adventure?" Zeke teased, following next to Marcus.

"We're on Mars," Marcus pointed out. "How much more adventure can you get?"

"Fair," Zeke yielded.

Having been quiet up until now, Miles spoke to Rubi. "The resistance was destroyed, our lives are at risk, they have his mother, people are suffering...!" His voice was kept low, despite the urgent tone. "And they're speaking so casual, joking!"

"There's always someone suffering or some looming threat," she whispered. "Focus too much on it, then it's hard to carry on."

Miles went silent again. It was hard for him to see anything but the fight, the struggle. It had been going on so long and had only gotten worse after the war. The defeat had been taken out on the citizens. He wished earth had finished the fight, rather than just banishing them to Mars. If earth had taken out the leader and the military, they could be living in peace now.

The heroes were hiding behind a rock formation, looking over at the prison. It was like a giant cage, having no solid walls to protect from the elements. The prisoners were forced to helplessly endure the bitter cold of Martian nights and the wicked dust storms that tore across the landscape. Guards were stationed around the perimeter, wearing heavy-duty cloaks. There was a metal box with windows by the prison for the guards to take shelter during a dust storm.

"I say we go for broke and free everyone, not just that man's wife and son," Marcus suggested, glaring at the offending structure before him.

Rubi grabbed a potato-sized rock and held it until it started glowing. She flung it straight at the shelter box, the rock crashing in through the window. Surprised yelps were heard before an explosion blew the windows out and damage the shelter box. Shouts were heard as the guards standing around the prison fence rushed toward the explosion.

"When were you going to mention that you could turn rocks into grenades?" Marcus asked rhetorically, mouth agape.

"When it became relevant," Rubi answered.

"Ah." Marcus returned his focus to the prison and the frantic guards. He launched over the boulders and dashed toward them. The guards began firing but Marcus zig-zagged from side to side. Electrically charged fists met each of the guards and toppled them to the ground.

The others, led by Rubi, took off for the prison fences. Rubi charged up a sizable fireball between her palms and fired at the fence at an angle, blasting a hole through it but missing everyone inside. The prisoners stood like statues, staring at the hole.

"Why aren't they escaping?" Zeke asked. "We took care of the guards. What're they waiting for?"

"They're afraid," Rubi answered.

"Of what? Us?" Zeke wondered as he grabbed the fence and started pulling to make the hole bigger.

"No," Miles replied. "They're afraid of what will happen to them if they escape and they're caught later. There isn't a safe place to escape to when the planet you live on is ruled by one government, especially when that government cares more about furthering its control than taking care of its people."

Zeke didn't respond back. It really was a dire situation. The people on earth knew conditions were bad here, but they didn't know the details. Plus, they assumed that all Chimera were on the same side. It was really only the government that hated earth and wanted to conquer it. The citizens seemed to not care anything about that. They only wanted freedom.

Marcus marched over to the prison fence, carrying one of the guard's guns. He stepped through the hole and made his way to the middle of the prison. "Listen to me!" he shouted, though all eyes were already on him. "If you just stay here, nothing will change! The Chimera military is strong and well-armed, but you—the people —outnumber them! If you all banded together, they would eventually lose! I'm not gonna lie to you, many of you will probably die just like the resistance did, but isn't it worth it to be free of this fear? Isn't it worth it to make a better place for your children?"

The prisoners were silent, just as they had been the whole time. They shifted their gaze to each other, their eyes wordlessly asking the same questions.

"Whoo, what a speech," Zeke commented as he strode up next to Marcus. "Don't forget why we're here, mate. The black-market monkey's family?"

"Are you... talking about my husband?" A lemur-therian stepped forward. Her fur was ruffled and matted, and her clothes were torn. Beside her was a young boy who appeared to be part monkey- and part lemur-therian. They matched the photos the man had shown them.

"Yes," Marcus answered. "He sent us to rescue you. So, you can come with us. We'll take you to him."

"Thank you, but..." The woman patted her son's head. "If we leave here and we're caught again, the next place will be... the head bioresearch facility. They'll conduct horrible experiments on us."

Marcus searched for what to say. How could he help these people to want to fight for themselves? How could he show them that it was possible to defeat the Chimera Regime? "Listen!" He turned to the others again. "I am from earth! I'm here because the Chimera Elite kidnapped my mother, Masumi Valko! My name is Dynamo! I fought the Chimera twenty years ago." Marcus had to be careful of what he said as he still couldn't remember much of his past beyond that dream he had. He only knew what he had pieced together from others. He also had to be careful not to make any promises that he couldn't keep. He may have been a soldier before, but that was then, and this was now. He didn't know the extent of his abilities and he certainly didn't know the extent of the Chimera military's power currently. It would be enough just to rescue his mother. He would see what else he could do in the process.

The prisoners came to an agreement and began filing out through the hole. They gathered in a group outside, not sure where to go. Going home wasn't an option and there wasn't a safe place to hide with the resistance gone.

"Nox," Marcus said as he exited the prison. "Can you look at the guard's guns and see if you can remove the GPS chips? It won't be enough for everyone, but it'll be something."

"Sure." Nox flew over to the downed guards and started working on taking the guns apart to get at the chips. Too bad Marcus hadn't thought of this earlier with the soldiers that were harassing that old man. They could've had some guns for themselves.

"Now what?" Zeke asked.

"We take these two back with us," Marcus answered, pointing at the lemur-therian and her son, "and get our IDs so we can get on the train and get my mom."

"Sounds so simple, but how much you wanna bet it won't be?" Zeke posed, an ironic smile on his face.

"Nothing." Marcus placed his fists on his waist.

Rubi stepped up to the two. "Miles has decided to stay with the prisoners and lead them. He will contact us if he finds out anything else concerning your mother."

"Alright, if that's what he wants to do." Marcus shrugged. "We should get going. It won't be long before someone notices what happened and sends more soldiers out."

Rubi nodded in agreement. They started heading back to the city after collecting Nox, who had finished removing the GPS chips from the guard's guns. They wondered how the ex-prisoners would fair and if they could become a new resistance. They were certainly already tough to be able to survive the harsh conditions of that prison camp.

The group, minus Miles, arrived in the city and made their way to the monkey-therian's secret hideaway. After a happy reunion with his wife and child, he handed over the fake IDs. After looking them over, they pocketed them. Miles' ID was left behind in case he decided to come get it on his own.

They left the hideaway and meandered through the city to throw off any suspicions.

Then they made their way to the train station and got in line. They swiped their IDs on the way in and found an out-of-the-way place to sit down. They had all already absolved to not speak during the trip, lest they say something that would give them away as being not from around here.

Marcus leaned against the wall; the side of his face pressed up against the window, watching as they left the station. This would be far more fascinating if it weren't for the circumstances that had brought him here, if it wasn't for the circumstances of the Martian people. He watched the scenery as they traveled, though they were going much too fast for him to make much out. He saw the expected rusty dirt and red rocks, but there were also some plants that one would expect to see in the desert. It was a shame that the terraforming of Mars a century ago had gone to waste. Making the formerly hostile planet habitable to humans was an amazing feat, yet it was now just home to the Chimera Regime and its oppressed people. Perhaps, one day, it could be reclaimed and be a second home to humanity and the therians.

After several stops, the train finally pulled into the station of the capitol. This city looked to be better off, cleaner and with richer folks. They were likely all loyal to the regime.

"We'll have to be careful here," Rubi whispered as if they hadn't needed to be careful before. "I know a place we can hide for now, until we find out where your mother is being held."

"Alright." Marcus gave a nod. "Lead the way."

CHAPTER 14

Marcus, Rubi, Zeke, Nox, and Marin were all holed up in a secret cave, the place Rubi had told them about. They had been hiding there for a couple of days now, nearly out of the food that the old man had given them and still with no leads to where Marcus' mother was being held. Marcus was brooding, annoyed by the fact that they had come so far and were so close, but still didn't know where to look.

Just when Marcus felt it was hopeless, Miles stepped in through the doorway, his clothing torn and his breath ragged. "I found... where they're holding... your mother," he said between gasps. "The main weapons development facility."

"You okay?" Marcus asked as he went to support Miles, who nodded. "Weapons development, not prison? That... makes me uneasy. Why there?"

"Don't know." Miles had managed to catch his breath, sitting down. "They make regular weapons there, but also bioweapons. I couldn't find out what they were planning, just that she was there. I barely managed to get away. I think... they let me get away."

"So, we're going to be walking right into a trap? That's just wonderful," Zeke griped.

"What choice do we have? There's no other way to get to her. We knew this was going to be hard," Marcus pointed out.

"Don't mean I have to like it."

"Fair enough." Marcus paused, considering their options. "They'll expect us to try to sneak in since that's the sensible thing to do. So, we'll have to do the insensible thing and rush in head-on and plow through."

"What?" Zeke questioned.

"I agree." Rubi stepped forward. "Marcus, Zeke, and I can rush the guards. After they've been distracted, Miles, Marin, and Nox can sneak in the other side to find Masumi."

"Sounds simple enough."

"It won't be easy," Rubi cautioned. "If it's a trap, the Elite will be waiting for us."

As the group approached the weapons facility, they split off. Marcus, Rubi, and Zeke went one way while Nox, Miles, and Marin went the other way. Marcus' group traveled faster than the other so that they'd get noticed first. Miles' group traveled slower and had their cloaks' camouflage feature active, blending into the Martian soil. The outside of the building was strangely devoid of guards, which further confirmed it was a trap. Unfortunately, the only way to get to Marcus' mother was to spring it.

Approaching the main doors, Marcus' group stopped. Expecting to have guards to fight, they hadn't planned on how to actually get in the building.

"You looking for a doorbell, mate? Just punch the thing in. Right?" Zeke thought it was simple enough.

"I don't know, I haven't tried punching in any doors yet." It struck Marcus as funny, or maybe ironic, that he hadn't yet tested the true limits of his strength yet. There hadn't really been time. Though he suspected that he would get the chance to soon.

"Let's both do it," Zeke suggested, holding up his fists. "I need to wear this suit in."

"Alright." Both Marcus and Zeke stood in front of the door, pulling back a fist. They thrust their arms forward, pounding their fists into the metal door. Two sizable dents were made, Marcus' being much bigger than Zeke's.

"No fair."

Marcus shrugged. "Android."

"Just keep punching 'til we get through." Zeke started punching in the door, Marcus quickly following suit. It wasn't long before it was punched open and the three slipped through.

Rubi took point, her superior senses working overtime to detect the slightest hint of danger. This was quite possibly her most dangerous mission yet. She'd destroyed warehouses but she'd never been in the primary weapons development facility. This was where people like Neva were born, where Randor got his extra power, where enemies of the Regime were tortured in inhumane experiments to make a better race of therians. Still, this time, she had help, including the help of a war hero. It was still hard for her to believe this android was Dynamo. He was much more down-to-earth than she had expected, having had expected someone more like a general.

Rubi raised her hand. Marcus and Zeke stopped in their tracks, keeping silent. Her ears twitched and she took a whiff of the air. "Not Elite. Footsteps sound like researchers, not soldiers." Indeed, the footsteps sounded casual, not like marching.

"I got this." Zeke ran off down the corner, yelling as soon as he saw the researchers. Startled, a few froze to the spot and a few turned and ran. Zeke clotheslined the ones frozen and took after the ones running.

"Is your friend... always like this?" Rubi asked, blinking in surprise at how he just ran off.

"Yeah? Pretty much." Marcus scratched the back of his neck. "We used to get into a lot of fights in high school. Mostly against bullies that were picking on the other kids, like Nox."

Rubi blinked a few more times before following after Zeke; Marcus followed her. They could hear screams and the sound of people being tossed against the wall. Marcus and Rubi arrived to find Zeke standing and all of the researchers unconscious.

"And I don't feel a bit bad tossing you crooks around," Zeke gloated. "Therians're supposed to be tougher than humans anyway, and you galahs do sick experiments on people so don't expect any mercy from me!"

"Someone's all worked up." Marcus stepped toward his friend, a smirk on his face and his arms crossed.

"Just 'cause they don't have my mum doesn't mean I'm not mad! They hurl our mate Nox too and I've been wanting to pay them back!" Zeke shook a fist for emphasis. "Not to mention attacking you."

"More are coming!" Rubi warned. "Chat later!"

"Right!" Marcus and Zeke charged off down the hall, itching to continue the fight. Rubi followed behind. This time, they ran into guards. Simple punches and kicks, Marcus' enhanced with electricity, were enough to fell them. Rubi used her pyrokinesis to redirect the plasma bolts away from Marcus and Zeke, and towards the guards. So much for the Chimera military, but they weren't wearing armor suits. It was also possible that they were ordered to go down easy to lure the heroes into a false sense of confidence. More guards came, speeding towards the heroes like a swarm of cockroaches. The three braced themselves for the onslaught.

Meanwhile, the other three were slipping through the facility undetected, checking each room as they passed by, unlocking them with a key card that Miles had stolen. "I don't like this," Nox groaned. "There should be some resistance, better security. This is too easy."

"You worry too much," Marin dismissed him. "They're busy dealing with Rubi and your friends."

"Don't be ungrateful," Miles cautioned. "Just take it. We're not going back."

"I wasn't saying we should, just that something's wrong. Just keep an ear out for any trouble, okay? We don't want them to get the drop on us," Nox insisted, still feeling uneasy.

"Says the guy with satellite dish ears," Miles remarked.

Nox's mouth was agape and he looked taken aback, but the bat had no comeback. Why had he agreed to do this dangerous mission? To come back to the place that took his parents from him? The place that he nearly died? He supposed he felt he owed it to Marcus, who came to his defense when the others picked on him, who became his friend. Marcus and Zeke were the only people Nox had. If they had gone off alone and died, Nox would be all alone and he couldn't bear the thought of that. So, he supposed, he had come here to die with his friends. All for one, and one for all.

"Picking up on anything?" Miles asked.

Nox's ears swiveled. "The sound of electricity there is very loud. That room has more machines in it than the others."

"Meaning...?" Miles questioned.

"I don't know," Nox answered exasperatedly. "Open the door."

Miles swiped the key card and the door opened. They stepped in, Marin turning on the light. All three gasped at the sight before them. Standing like statues were dozens, upon dozens of robots. They all had the appearance of humanoid felines, but not one of the types seen among the therians. They were modeled after saber-tooth tigers, the telltale dagger-like teeth protruding from their mouths.

"W-where did they get those?" Marin asked, trembling.

"It's... an army." Nox backed up. "We... should check the next room."

"Agreed." Miles started backing up as well. "Marin!" Miles called out, having lost track of her. He heard someone trip and fall. "Marin!"

"I'm okay!" The badger got up, having tripped over one of the robot's feet, and started running back to the others. Behind her, they could see the robot's eyes light up.

"It's time to go!" Nox shouted as he tore out of the room and down the hall. Miles and Marin were hot on his heels. The robot followed them out of the room and began stalking down the hall. Then they could hear more metallic footsteps. Had all the robots been activated? This had quickly gone from bad to worse. They couldn't hope to fend them all off, even with Nox and Marin in armor. After several blind turns, Miles' group ran into Marcus' group, who had just finished taking out another squad of guards.

"Fancy meeting you here," Marcus deadpanned. Looking behind the three, he saw the squadron of saber-tooth tiger robots hot on their tails. "Looks like you brought company."

"What the bloody heck are those?!" Zeke exclaimed. "Yeah, nah, I did not sign up for this!"

Rubi charged forward, dodging around the others, and heading straight for the robots. She held out her hand and materialized a glowing orange spear made of plasma. Reaching the first robot, she sent the head of the plasma spear right through its chest, then spun around, sending it into the wall.

"Wait, she can do that? Since when could she do that?" Zeke questioned, approaching hysterics.

Marcus shrugged. "She's just full of surprises."

"You got that right." Zeke couldn't help but feel like the only normal one here, a regular human among these super-powered titans, and that was with him being a cyborg. Though his bionic arm, lung, and heart weren't made to be super strong, rather, they were designed to mimic the real thing. Zeke's bionic arm didn't make him able to win every arm-wrestling competition, though he wasn't too shabby. These people were several times stronger, faster, and tougher than he was.

"C'mon!" Marcus shouted. "Rubi needs our help." He rushed off toward the hoard robots, electrified fists at the ready. Marin had already taken off after her.

Zeke charged off after him, wondering how he would fair against the robots. Nox followed, flying overhead to deal with them from another angle. The bat dive-bombed the robots, kicking their heads before flying back up out of reach. He did this several times before one caught him by the wing and hurled him into the wall.

"Nox!" Marcus and Zeke shouted in unison, rushing over to their friend.

"You alright, mate?" Zeke asked.

"Your wing..." Marcus' fingers brushed across Nox's wing, which flinched at the slight touch. It looked horribly mangled, certainly broken.

"I'll... be fine. Just worry about the robots." Nox's voice was strained.

"Hey, think you can go find my mom while we're dealing with these things?" Marcus asked. It would be better if Nox stayed away from the fighting.

"Yeah, I can do that." There was no way Nox could say no.

"Thanks, buddy. Take Miles and Marin with you." Marcus stood up, signaling the gerbil-therian and badger-therian to come over, explaining when she arrived. Miles, Marin, and Nox took off down the hallway.

Turning back around to face the robots, Marcus clenched his fists. "You..." Marcus stepped forward. "...will..." He dashed off. "...pay for that!"

As he rushed toward one of the robots, a sword materialized into his hand in a flash of light. He plunged the crackling blue blade into the robot.

"Since when-" Zeke started but cut himself off. "Never mind." There was no use asking. Marcus was as full of surprises as Rubi was. Zeke simply jogged back into the fray. The sooner they beat these robots, the sooner they could get back to their mission. He hoped Nox and Marin wouldn't run into any resistance since it all seemed to be right here.

The battle raged on. Marcus tore through the robots with his newly discovered sword. Rubi stabbed them with her plasma spear and melted them with her flames. Zeke simply punched them or dodged their punches, so they'd punch each other.

"Don't reckon you can make me one of those spears?" Zeke asked when he found himself back-to-back with Rubi.

"No," she answered, stabbing a robot in the neck. "You'd burn your hands."

"Oh." It was too bad. If only Nox had had time to construct weapons for them as well.

The three were making short work of the robots but felt close to being overwhelmed. It was not easy to keep up with tireless machines for these were clearly not androids. They reacted not to pain nor with fear. They were like mobile statues, no more than automatons.

Meanwhile, Nox, Miles, and Marin were close to their goal. They neared one of the central labs. "Here." Nox stopped at door. "There are people here."

Miles swiped the key card and the door slid open.

"Marcus," Nox said into the comm-link in his helmet. "You might want to come over here. We found her."

"Really?" Marcus responded. "I'm on my way."

It didn't take Marcus long to arrive at Nox's location, though he did get delayed by a few more guards, which he promptly took out. The android imagined that his kill count today didn't even come close to what it was as Dynamo during the war. He wasn't sure how comfortable he was with this, though he knew that they were the enemy and had likely killed far more innocence than that. They wouldn't hesitate to kill him, his friends, or his mother.

Nox simply gestured for Marcus to enter the room. When he did, his eyes widened in shock at what he saw before him. It was his mother, leaning over a robot of the same model that they had been fighting. She was assembling it! His mother also had a blank, hollow stare, just like Rubi had had before during their fight at the convention. Marcus' focus shifted to see Neva standing behind his mother. It was clear now what was going on. Neva had been ordered to mind-control his mother, brainwashing her into creating this army of robots, robots that they likely planned on using to attack earth.

Marcus charged to attack Neva, but he was knocked off his feet and into the wall by a sonic scream. He looked up to see Randor entering the room from another door.

"Why do you want to save this human?" Randor asked, his eyes piercing into Marcus'.

"What do you mean? She's my mom, she created me." Marcus had gotten to a knee but didn't plan to stand up yet, lest he just get knocked back down again.

A clawed finger pointed at Marcus. "Surely, you've figured it out by now." Randor paced closer, his toothy grin ever-present, and a hand behind his back. "Our pasts are intertwined, you and I. We fought against each other several times during the war. You could say we're rivals. When Father told me you were still alive, I was excited at the opportunity to face you again and prove my superiority once and for all. Kidnapping your "mother" to build us a robot army was just a bonus."

Wow, Rubi was right, Marcus thought. I didn't have to say hardly anything to get him monologuing. Still, what could he do with that when Randor wouldn't look away?

"I was really hoping to fight Dynamo. As Marcus, you're not ready yet to give me a real fight, but you're in the way now so I have no choice." Randor charged forward, finally pulling his arm from behind his back, revealing a sword. It was of unusual design, the blade being wide and made of metal, with only the edge glowing yellow.

Marcus rolled out of the way to dodge the first blow, which made the sound of crackling lightning upon hitting the wall. Using his own sword, Marcus blocked the second attack. Randor screamed, sending

Marcus back, but he managed to stay on his feet this time. Marcus charged forward only to have Randor dodge to the side and trip him. Marcus tucked in and turned his fall into a somersault, getting back to his feet and turning around in time to block another swing from Randor's sword.

Nox, Miles, and Marin could only watch in terror, knowing none of them stood a chance against Randor. It's why the resistance had always sent Rubi to handle the Elite while they carried out the mission. They really were in a whole other league.

Rubi and Zeke finally arrived, having finished dealing with the remaining robots. Quickly assessing the situation, Rubi slipped into the room and headed straight for Neva, taking her down with a roundhouse kick.

Broken of her connection to Neva, Masumi looked about in numb confusion. She wasn't being directly controlled by Neva, but her mind still weighed heavy from the brainwashing. Masumi was barely aware of Zeke and Nox surrounding her and leading her away from the battle.

"I'll stay out here and keep an eye on her." Zeke helped Masumi down slowly to sit on the floor.

"Okay, I'll go see what I can do." Nox ran back into the room, not sure what he could do with a broken wing fragmenting his focus. Nox never had taken Marcus and Zeke up on their offer to teach him how to fight, preferring to study or tinker. Now he was regretting that.

The room was in shambles, cracks and scorch marks on the walls, floor, and ceiling; all the equipment upturned and broken.

The combatants weren't fairing much better, both breathing heavily. Marcus' armor was cracked and had various gouges from Randor's sword; electricity sparked wildly from the holes in his armor. Randor's state was about the same, blood soaking his fur and clothing, a few claws broken off.

"You... ready to give up?" Randor asked, maintaining bravado through ragged breaths.

"I was... about to ask you the same," Marcus replied, a smirk on his face.

Randor laughed, blood dripping from his mouth. "Refusing to admit defeat, huh? Heh, we're so alike, you and I, you could say we were brothers."

"I'm nothing like you!" Marcus roared, charging at Randor and body-slamming him into the wall. "I could never be like you!" Marcus punched Randor repeatedly in the gut. "You're a monster!" Ending his barrage, Marcus stepped back, allowing Randor to fall to the ground. The wolf-therian breathed short, shallow breaths.

Azura finally arrived, having taken a detour to fetch the portal device in case things got dicey. Peeking into the room, she immediately noticed Rubi frozen in place like a statue. Neva was lying on the floor, a hand outstretched towards Rubi. The red fox-therian had fallen victim to Neva's brain-lock technique, just as Azura had earlier. She was immobile for the moment, but Azura could see Rubi's muscles twitching and knew she wouldn't be held for long. Surveying the rest of the room, her eyes widened upon seeing Randor flat on the floor, Marcus standing over him with sword in hand. Randor was struggling to get up but kept falling back down, hands slipping on his own blood. Heart racing, Azura frantically looked around, trying to come up with a plan. Blasting Marcus with her flames would hit Randor as well and they were too close together to open a portal. From the corner of her eye, she noticed Masumi and Zeke just outside the door. She dashed towards them, grabbing Masumi by the shirt, and tossing her back into the room.

"Hey!" Zeke lunged at her. "You leave her alone!"

"Why don't you make me?" Azura winked, dodging Zeke's punch, and jumping back into the room.

"Don't think I won't!" Zeke followed her, not even considering the fact she could roast him alive.

Marcus looked over his shoulder at the commotion, noticing the portal. He tensed.

A squad of robots like the ones before marched into the room, having been following Azura there but being much slower than her. They apprehended the others, maintaining tight grips on Miles, Marin, and Nox's arms. Miles didn't resist. Marin struggled, wanting to take them all on. Nox stared blankly into space, his glimmer of hope gone.

"Like our new soldiers curtesy of your mother?" Azura teased. "We call them smilodroids and they're more than enough to conquer earth with, don't you think?"

"They didn't seem so tough to us." Marcus folded his arms, trying to maintain composure and a clear head.

"Yes, well, you're an exception. The other earthlings won't find them so easy to deal with," Azura assured, grabbing Masumi and tossing her in the portal.

As Marcus stared in horror, Azura kicked Zeke into the portal too. With a shout, Marcus lunged forward and into the portal. Wherever his mother and friend were being sent, he had to be with them.

Rubi finally broke free from Neva's mental grasp, blasting her with fire as she took off for the portal, dashing inside.

Marin wrestled out of the smilodroid's grasp, running for the portal. "Rubi! Wait for me!" She dashed into the portal just as it was closing, disappearing in a purple flash.

Randor struggled to his feet as Azura approached. "Why did you do that?" he burst, eyes burning.

"The Chimera Regime needs its only heir alive."

"I could have beaten him!" Randor sputtered, then collapsed to the floor.

Azura called for medical assistance, standing by Randor as she waited.

Nox's eyes were wide in horror. He was all alone now, his friends gone off to who knows where. His mind screamed at the thought of returning to Chimera prison, or worse. He knew what was in store and was sure Miles did too.

At the exit location of the portal, Rubi fell on her hands and knees, sobbing. Marcus knelt beside her. "What's wrong? What happened to Marin? Where is she?"

The badger was nowhere to be seen.

"She's gone!" Rubi bawled.

"What... do you mean?" Marcus whispered.

"She was in the portal when it closed. It's like a black hole. Anything still inside when it's closed is... crushed into oblivion!" Rubi threw herself into Marcus' arms, continuing to sob. He held her tightly, wishing to take her pain away.

After what felt like an eternity, but was actually just a short while, Zeke spoke up. "Um, not to be insensitive here, but... where are we?"

At the question, Marcus looked up and around, taking in the landscape. They seemed to be in a small clearing in a forest, but it wasn't like any forest he'd ever seen. The trees appeared almost like palm trees but with thicker leaves, which were almost black and covered in a purple fuzz. The foliage close to the ground resembled ferns and had the same purple fuzz. Even the grass was purple. Marcus and Zeke looked up through the hole in the treetops above them at the sun. It looked smaller than it was supposed to be and was a deep orange. They caught glimpses of strange creatures traveling through the trees that looked like wyverns the size of bats.

"Woah." Marcus' mouth was agape. "What is this place?"

Rubi stood up, facing away from the others. When she looked back over her shoulder, her skin was charcoal gray and there were orange markings on her face like tiny flicks of flame. "This place is my home planet: Ahkmar."

Randor had been taken to the bioresearch section of the building. He had been placed in a special chemical vat meant to heal his wounds as he slept. The researchers were frantically overlooking his vitals to make sure everything was going well. Randor had taken quite a beating, but it was nothing he couldn't recover from.

A white wolf-therian stepped into the room. All eyes were on him immediately.

"A-alpha Amarok!" the head researcher, a rat-therian, addressed him. "All is going well. His wounds are healing quite nicely. Are... are you sure you want to go through with this? It's a risky procedure and there's no guarantee of success."

"I understand and I am very sure," Amarok bellowed.

"Yes, sir!" The rat-therian returned to his work.

Everyone nervously continued working. The Alpha's presence was an imposing one for he did not tolerate failure in any capacity. Even the smallest error was punished severely.

"My, my," a sultry voice drifted through the door. Azura stepped in. "I've heard of buying a new wardrobe when the old ones wear out, but this?"

Amarok turned to face her, a snarl on his face. "You-"

Azura casually walked up to him, not at all afraid like the researchers. "Don't worry, your secret's safe with me. I'm loyal to the regime, not Randor, and as the leader of the regime, I'm loyal to you."

Amarok's snarl faded as he considered her words. He paced back over to the vat that held Randor, who was as unconscious as before.

"Very well. You will assist me as you've assisted Randor. You can start by taking the Elite and overseeing the operation on Ahkmar."

"As you command." Azura saluted, then left the room to carry out her new orders.

Amarok turned to the head researcher. "I have some things to take care of. Contact me when you are ready."

"Yes, sir!" the rat-therian assured.

Amarok left the room.

The researchers continued their work, relatively more relaxed without the Alpha's presence, but not by much. They began preparing the room for the procedure.

In the chemical healing vat, unnoticed by everyone in the room, Randor's ear twitched and the faintest snarl crept on his face.

FIN

Made in the USA
Columbia, SC
19 October 2022

69722542R00195